THE GREATEST MANN

IN

THE WORLD

A NOVEL

Matt Micros

Heroes are easily recognized. Just look for the ordinary person who steps forward into an extraordinary circumstance while everyone else stands still.

<u>*Also by Matt Micros*</u>

~Five Days~

~The Knights of Redemption~

~The Chameleon~

~Nick Nelson Was Here~

TABLE OF CONTENTS

THE GREATEST MANN
IN THE WORLD

"Children aren't the only ones who need heroes."
Tamora Pierce

This book is a work of fiction.
No part of the contents relate to any real person or
persons living or dead. No events depicted actually
happened or are implied to have happened.

I
~SNOWIFORNIA~

What if you awoke one morning to find that everything you had known to be true and normal in your life, suddenly no longer was? What if with no advance notice whatsoever, the sun began to rise in the west and set in the east? What if on a random December day, it began snowing in Southern California and didn't stop for four months? What if at that same time, the temperature in Milford, Connecticut soared into the 80's? What if Seattle had four straight months of complete darkness followed by 20 hours a day of sunshine for three months? What if the United States was involved in a endless war that when combined with the environmental shift had caused the country to fall into a deep recession; with gas prices at an all-time high, the stock market at a 40 year low, with giant corporations going out of business on what seemed like a daily basis. What if? What if? What if?

* * * *

The day began typically enough for mid-December in the nation's capital; cold, dark and grey with a heavy fog that had settled into the district so thick that you practically had to wipe it from your face. People weaved their way through the pedestrian traffic as if everyone else had been put in front of them solely to impede them from where they were headed.   The mood in the country was as gloomy as the weather.

Meanwhile, on the second floor conference room in a building on the corner of 11th Street and Pennsylvania Avenue, key members of the Democratic National Committee were fast at work deciding what was in the best interest of the American people—without bothering to actually ask them what they wanted.

It was a room filled with castoffs and wannabes. Life for these people, with very few exceptions, had not turned out as they had hoped when they were younger, and they were making certain now that they had the opportunity, to inflict payback on anyone whose life *hadn't* been an unhappy and veritable mess in their youth.

Dick Stoops was the unabashed leader of the group, but certainly not for his looks or charm. He was mostly bald, sporting the half globe, with hair on the sides and back of his head. His voice was deep and imposing, with the ability to drown out nearly any sound in its path.

"Did anyone see The Post this morning?" he asked almost rhetorically.

A woman in her late 40's, pretty beneath her red pantsuit and white blouse, chimed in. "They're saying that as long as we put forth a woman or a minority as Huber's running mate, the election is ours to lose."

"And they're right," Stoops answered. "Which is why we *will* put forth one or the other. Our job over the next several days is to talk the also-rans out of the race."

An African American man in his early 40's, who didn't seem at all bothered by their political pandering, threw in his two cents. "Do we have anything to offer them?"

"Such as?"

"Cabinet positions, future considerations..." the man responded.

"Jesus Christ, Ron. This isn't the NFL draft."

"I understand that, but Rick Jeremiah has plenty of money, and isn't afraid to spend it. He could drag the nomination all the way to the convention floor if he wanted to."

Stoops mulled it over for about ten seconds, which was generally the amount of time he allotted to even the most important of decisions. He hated being strong-armed into doing anything, but was also smart enough to know when to retreat.

"Ok. Tell Jeremiah he'll have a cabinet position if he withdraws and throws his support behind Huber. Tell the others to fuck off honorably or the next job they have in politics will be as a Lunch Monitor at a middle school in Poughkeepsie."

There was a noticeable chuckle in the room. It was clear that most people there loved the fact that they wielded so much power.

"What we need to figure out is who would be a better compliment to Huber. O'Bannon?

Or Calvert? The African American? Or the woman? For that matter, are we sure that Huber is the person we want to put on top of the ticket? Which will play better? Thoughts?" Stoops said.

If Dan Holmes wasn't the youngest in the room, he was close to it. He looked be in his early 30's, clean-cut, well-spoken and passionate. Everything the rest of them were not. He cleared his throat before speaking, knowing full well that what he was about to say wouldn't be well received. "Isn't that for the public to decide?" he managed to spit out.

Stoops seemed more amused than annoyed. "Son, I know you're new to this game, so here's how it's played. Ninety-eight percent of the population is made up of morons who couldn't pick their nose without instructions. So it's up to us to tell them how to think based on the information we decide to leak to the press."

"Doesn't that kind of go against the very principles of a Democracy?"

There was a collective gasp in the room, followed by awkward silence, until—

"What the hell's going on out there?!" Ron exclaimed, pointing out the window for emphasis.

"The sun's out. It has happened before," Stoops answered sarcastically.

In fact, it was, having suddenly burst through the clouds like a brick thrown through a wet paper bag.

"Not just that. Why is everyone taking their jackets off?"

"They're warm?"

"When I left my house this morning, it was 12 degrees outside. They said the high was going to be 27 today."

"So the weather forecaster was wrong. That would be so shocking."

"Fifty degrees wrong?"

The people outside were wiping the sweat from their brows and looking to the heavens as if they suddenly found themselves standing beneath a giant hair dryer on the highest possible setting.

Someone slid open a window and stuck his arm out. "It's really warm. Like *really* warm," the man said.

* * * *

Three hundred miles away in Milford, Connecticut, Bernice and Joe Kreps took an unexpected stroll along the beach. They had lived in the same house directly across from the Long Island Sound for the past 37 years—which was the same length of time as their marriage. They had raised two children in that house, and seen four grandchildren walk through its doors. The house itself was a three bedroom cottage, with hardwood floors throughout and a screened in front porch, from which they spent many a night watching people walk along the beach. *Quaint* and *comfortable* were perhaps the two most apt words used to describe the home, although their son came home one day from high school and announced that their house looked like the guesthouse to one of the million dollar estates that sandwiched it on both sides. They laughed when he said it because they knew it was true, and because they also knew they would never be able to afford to live there on an electrician and teacher's salaries if they were just starting out today. That is also what made them appreciate it as much as they did. Bernice and Joe loved taking long walks along the water and into town. They loved the little corner delis and pizza shops. And they loved that on sunny days, the light woke them up by shining brightly through the many blind free windows.

Winters had grown increasingly difficult as they grew older, and on more than one occasion, they looked into buying a second home in Florida, but simply couldn't afford it. And when December 4 began with bright, blue skies and temperatures rising through the 70's, no one appreciated it more than the Kreps.

"I mean, we're retired, so it makes sense that we're out here today," Joe told his wife while they strolled along the walking path while dozens of college age people—some wearing Yale t-shirts--played football, volleyball and Frisbee on the beach. "But what is everyone else doing out here? Don't they have school? Or jobs?"

"Not everyone thinks it's a sin to take a day off once in a while," his wife answered.

"Not taking a day off is what put two kids through college."

"You did have some help, you know."

"Yeah, but you were a teacher. Between summers and sick days, you had nearly three months off a year."

"Don't even start with me," she said.

"I'm just teasing," Joe laughed. "But I still don't understand what all these people are doing here. That's the problem with today's society. They have no work ethic."

"You better be careful," Bernice warned, "or instead of calling you Grampy Joe, our grandchildren are going to start calling you Grumpy Joe."

Just then, three boys on bicycles whizzed past, along with two girls on roller blades, the last of which bumped Joe as she went by. "Damn teenagers," he grumbled as his wife rolled her eyes.

Across town, Professor Cummings looked out at what was supposed to be a class of forty-eight students and saw only seven. "What's the deal, ladies and gentlemen? Is it class cut day?" he asked to silence. The students that were in the room were there for a reason. They had no social skills whatsoever. It was the quietest class he ever remembered teaching.

"Tom, were you missing a lot of students today?" he asked another professor he passed on his way back to his office.

"Quite a few," was the response.

"I was missing 11 in Physics and 48 in Microbiology," Cummings lamented.

"Must be the weather. Although I'm not sure you can blame the weather for Microbiology," Tom laughed.

"But we have exams in a week, and this is *Yale*," Cummings said.

"I'm sure they'll show up as soon as the weather turns lousy again," Tom answered before adding, "When is it going to turn back by the way?"

"I just checked it and the weather pattern shows sunny and warm the rest of the week."

"Strange pattern for December wouldn't you say? Did you hear it's snowing in Southern California?"

"It's got to be the winds of El Nino," Cummings said while shaking his head. He was easily perturbed by anything out of the norm. He was especially perturbed by anything he should understand but didn't.

II
~UNDER THE COVER OF DAY~

*M*ost bachelors placed their alarm clock just out of reach so that they were literally forced to get out of bed to turn it off. Married people, at least the considerate ones, left it close enough so they could turn it off with as little disturbance to their other halves as possible. James Carr went one step further. He never used his alarm clock, but instead wore a watch to bed every night. He would set the watch alarm to vibrate, and more often than not, he was gone without his wife missing a moment's sleep. On this day, after taking a longer shower than usual, he swigged a wide glass of orange juice, and swallowed two pieces of buttered toast almost whole, before kissing his wife goodbye gently on the cheek.

He was used to driving to the country club in the dark. With the exception of late June, it was nearly always dark at 5:45am. James was the nearly retired President of the Pacific National Bank, who managed to keep PNB afloat when many of the nation's largest banks and lenders went under. He was a financial wizard that had made many a family, including his own, extremely wealthy, but his true passion was golf.

"A bad day of golf is better than a good day of just about anything else," he was prone to say. Set to retire from his 9 to 9 job at the end of the year, he was to the Seattle golf community what Hootie Johnson was to Augusta National. He was the Chairman of the West Pacific Country Club and for nearly two decades, weather permitting, he began every day with a round of golf before going into the job that paid the bills.

The chill in the air forced James to grab an extra sweater and heavier jacket for this morning's round. He was a bit surprised to find the club's parking lot nearly empty when he pulled in. "Sissies," he said to himself with a pleased smile.

He was greeted with, "Good morning, Mr. Carr," by the young man who placed his clubs on a waiting cart.

"Not very many purists this morning, eh, Rick?"

"Not many at all," Rick answered. "Just maybe 15 or so."

The people in question sipped coffee in the bar area as they waited for the fog to lift.

"Morning, James," the members of his foursome said when he walked in.

"Gents," he said with a nod. "Nice day for a round."

They nodded, because they knew he truly believed that was the case, even though it was still dark out and the temperature couldn't have been more than 30 degrees.

"Seem a little dark for 7am?" one of them

asked no one in particular.

"Probably the fog," someone answered.

An hour later, it was still dark, and it had begun to snow. Snow in Seattle was not unheard of, but was unusual, as temperatures even in the winter averaged in the upper 40's.

"Doesn't look like we're going to get this one in," a man sighed.

"Looks that way," James replied sadly.

As they left for their cars and their real jobs, James found it somewhat strange that at 8:30am, save for the reflection of the white snowflakes off the lights, it was still as dark as midnight. When two o'clock also came and went in darkness, James checked the Internet to see if he had missed some sort of solar eclipse. When he realized he hadn't, he checked the television for some sort of explanation. But no one had one. It was a day without any daylight. For James Carr, it was like a year without a Santa Claus.

Meanwhile, at the offices of Electrical Wholesalers Incorporated, a day without daylight was like Christmas come early for Jimmy Davis. He just didn't realize it yet.

"Those damn new light bulbs last too damn long," his boss bellowed.

"Isn't that a good thing?" Jimmy asked.

"Look, there's no easy way to say this, so here it is. I've got a bottom line to meet, and there's only two ways I'm going to be able to do it. One is to increase sales. But that's not likely to happen with these new bulbs, because people won't have to buy them as often. The other way is to cut expenses. Which means..."

Jimmy finished his sentence for him. "...cutting back on your sales force."

"Unfortunately," his boss nodded. "Look, you've done a great job here for the past five years."

"Seven actually."

"Seven. But if I don't meet the bottom line, I'm the one who's going to be out of a job."

"How long do I have?"

"Two weeks."

"Two weeks?! Dennis, I have a family to support. Can't you at least give me a month to either bring up the numbers or find another job?" Jimmy asked.

Dennis thought it over. "Hmmm," he thought out loud before responding as magnanimously as he could, "I guess I could do that."

"Thanks," Jimmy grumbled, as he immediately thought of how he was going to break the news to his wife. He had received a temporary stay of execution, but it would take a lot more than the Governor to save him next time. He would need help from a much higher being.

III
~A TALE OF TWO PEOPLE~

*F*rom the moment Sumner Stein tabbed him to be the next President of Sunshine Valley Studios, Jerry Weinberg knew he was stepping out of the frying pan and into the fire. Sumner hadn't gotten to where he was in the world—one of the 20 wealthiest people in the country—without stepping on a few necks during his ascent.

Jerry preferred the more subtle approach of having people hoist him upwards rather than climbing over them. It had worked well for him. He started his post collegiate world in the mailroom at the top talent agency in Hollywood, the agency that Sumner founded. Always on the lookout for new talent, Sumner eyed the kid in the mailroom who was polite, but confident; sensitive of other people's feelings, but not overly sensitive regarding his own. Jerry was soon promoted to a desk, also known as becoming a Junior Agent, working with Sumner's highest profile clients. Make no mistake, Sumner called all the shots while the kid learned the ropes, but the kid was only too happy to soon be a 25 year-old full partner in the company, instead of delivering giant pink teddy bears to the youngest daughters of a client or studio head, which is what he had been doing before being plucked from the mailroom.

Jerry eventually became the 2nd most powerful man in Hollywood, ascending to numero uno when Sumner retired and named Jerry to succeed him. It wasn't an easy decision leaving his comfort zone, but after years of watching Academy Award shows where his clients thanked everyone they'd ever met *except* their agent, he began to question the worth of his job. He had made more money than he could spend in two lifetimes, but he was tired of selling other people's work. He wanted to make something. He wanted to create something. And when one of his former employees left a lucrative position at the agency to become a high school athletic director back east, the die had been cast. His employee's departing comment had rattled around Jerry's head like a pinball endlessly caroming off the bumpers.

If you asked 100 people what movie had the biggest influence on their life, most people would struggle for an answer, but if you asked those same people which teacher had the biggest influence, their answer would take about two seconds.

Teaching was out of the question because it didn't pay enough, so when Sumner came calling, Jerry saw no choice but to accept. Instead of being a salesman, he would now be on the creative side. His biggest issue was that he couldn't just make movies *he* wanted to see. He needed to make them for the masses, and for that he needed to have his finger on the pulse of the idiots of society, because after all, they were the ones who frequented the theatres. The result was an endless string of trashy superhero films, and sequels to movies that weren't very good to begin with. He also needed to stay one step ahead of the curve. With on demand at home growing and movie theatres closing what seemed weekly, marketing and staying on budget was more crucial than ever before. As he looked out his office bay window and saw snow coming down in Los Angeles for the first time in 53 years splattering onto the pavement; he saw dollar signs vanishing before his very eyes.

"What do you mean they've shut down production for the day?!" Jerry bellowed.

"It's snowing, Jerry," his second in command answered matter-of-factly. Charlie Walsh was not easily intimidated, nor thin-skinned, which made him perfect for his job.

"I can see that it's snowing. I'm neither blind, nor a moron. They can create a sinking Titanic in a bathtub, but they can't create a little sunshine?"

"They can create sunshine. They just can't stop it from snowing."

"Well, have them shoot their interior shots on the sound stage. Or have them rewrite the script and set it in Aspen. They're already two weeks behind schedule. We can't afford to lose another day."

"I will pass that along, but I think a rewrite might create some difficulties for wardrobe."

"In my next life I want to be a weatherman," Jerry grumbled. "It's the only job in the country where you make a lot of money for being wrong all the time."

Idiots."

* * * *

In contrast, at that very moment 3,000 miles away back in Connecticut, the weather was perfect, and Nick Lawson couldn't have been more miserable. After finally stepping out of the rather sizeable shadow of his best friend with a successful business of his own, that very business was now being threatened by the unforeseen shift in the weather. Eighty degrees and sunshine was wonderful for surfers, but not so much if you were trying to fill an indoor soccer facility.

Nick and his friend had gone to school together from 3rd grade through their high school graduation. They played football and basketball together. They were both good students. But whereas Nick was good at a lot of things, John lived in the spotlight. Nick, on the other hand, worked behind the scenes. Whenever John's picture was on the front page of the newspaper, Nick was usually the person who he had his arm around just out of frame.

They got along famously. Nick was proud of his best friend's accomplishments. He had an entire wall devoted to him in his office, whether it was sports clippings, a magazine cover, or a movie poster for a movie that almost was. And his best friend admired Nick's ability to *march to the beat of his own drum.*

The two friends used to joke that the difference in their respective legacies was about six inches. That was the length John dove into the end zone after picking up a fumble to win the high school football state championship his senior year. It was also the distance away Nick had been when he fumbled while reaching for the goal line. "If I were only a couple inches taller or you were a couple of inches shorter, both of our lives would have been completely different," Nick joked.

"If my Aunt Matilda had balls, she'd be my uncle," John would shoot back, and they would both break into hysterical laughter, while John's mother chastised them for being crude.

After graduation, Nick veered off in a different direction than the Ivy League school John was headed to and went to Notre Dame, where he knew his athletic career would be mostly confined to club and intramural teams. He instead spread his wings by joining the Young Republicans, and chairing the Business Leaders of America. After graduating with a degree in Finance, Nick ignored his parents advice and used his portion of the money his grandmother had left him to open a restaurant with two friends. Six months later, both of his partners were engaged and Nick was left to run the place by himself—which was exactly what his parents had warned him about. Six months after that, he bought his partners out, essentially paying them for his having done all the work for the past year.

By that time, the restaurant was turning a profit, but he had little or no time to himself. When a real estate mogul came in and offered him three times what they had paid for the property, he sold it, and in the process learned the real money was in buying and selling real estate. It didn't matter what your business was. The property was the important thing.

In the meantime, after graduating from Yale as a two-time All-American football player, John was struggling to find himself. He was putting his Ivy League education to work as a bartender at a dive beach bar in Southern California, when Nick arrived unannounced to give him a much needed kick in the pants. It wasn't long before John was back on top of the world, only to walk away from it all and drift back into a life of relative obscurity as a high school administrator not far from where they had grown up. Nick followed him back east and continued investing in real estate, buying two duplexes and renting out both sides of them. The rent more than paid for his mortgage, and after three years, he turned a profit of nearly half a million dollars when he sold them. He then bought an office building in New Haven and leased it out to several corporations. The building had paid for itself within five years. And yet Nick wasn't happy. He hated the fact that he wasn't *creating* anything. So he bought a warehouse and started his indoor soccer arena. It was a great idea on paper. Participation in youth soccer was at an all-time high. For girls especially, soccer was the most rapidly growing sport. What Nick hadn't counted on was Mother Nature skipping winter and heading straight for summer. If the weather continued that way, his business would be worthless.

"Excuse me," a man said while Nick sat in the otherwise empty office.

"What can I do for you?" Nick answered, snapping out of his daydream.

"Not sure what your hours are, but a group of us work the second shift at the plastic factory down the road, and we'd like to rent the field if possible from midnight to 1:00am a couple of nights a week."

Nick quickly did the math in his head. The rental would barely make a dent in his mortgage which was due in three weeks and would mean a couple of late nights. But it was also one of the appealing aspects to opening the business in the first place. He had envisioned people coming there as an escape from their everyday lives.

"Why not?" he answered.

"Can we book it up for the next six weeks?" the man asked.

Nick paused a moment before responding this time. He might not still be in business in six weeks. "Why don't we start with three and go from there?"

IV
~THE UNIFIED PARTY~

*D*an Holmes was an idealistic Williams College grad where he majored in political science, with an eye towards law school. But when a friend asked him to run his campaign for Student Body President, he became so intrigued with the process, that law school became a distant memory. He loved the idea of making a bad situation better. Loved the idea of writing stirring speeches that would invigorate people who normally didn't care for much of anything. He was definitely a behind the scenes guy—all substance and no flash. Unfortunately, that didn't play well on the modern college campus and they lost the election to two guys who wrote their slogans on pieces of notebook paper with crayons and stuck them to trees all over campus.

We don't wear socks.
Our mother thinks you should vote for us.
We only shave for dances.
Real men wear shorts in the winter.
Free beer at our election party.

And so on... They didn't even have the decency to remove the fringes from the papers first.

Disappointed but not disillusioned, Dan knew that college life was as far from the real world as Anchorage was from Bangor, Maine, and the defeat only made him more motivated than ever to prove that substance was what mattered. Although he described himself as socially liberal and fiscally conservative, he joined the Democratic Party because he thought it would be easier to pull the liberal left toward the center, than the conservative right anywhere but further right. After all, even liberals liked money.

It didn't take long for him to see that political parties were more or less organized crime families, with half the people making backhanded deals to line their own pockets, while the other half stood behind a platform, even though they didn't even agree with half the ideas behind it. He grew more and more frustrated by the day, even as he continued to ascend the ranks within the party as its top speechwriter. And after leaving the meeting that December morning, he knew it was time for a change. He wanted to believe again, and he was pretty certain that it wouldn't happen there.

* * * *

Dan walked into the Capital Grille and joined one of the other young men from the earlier meeting at DNC Headquarters. Peter Cook was about the same age--dark hair, glasses, nice suit, with spit shined shoes.

"Why do you always have to get into it with Stoops?" Peter asked while ripping apart a warm roll.

"Because this isn't what I signed on for, Pete. I don't want to support someone because the Democratic Party tells me I should. I want to support a candidate because I agree with them on the issues; because I believe in them as a person."

"But you're on the fast track. If you can manage to keep your mouth shut, you might just find yourself as the Press Secretary at the White House someday."

"Doesn't keeping your mouth shut kind of go against what a Press Secretary is supposed to do?" Dan laughed.

"A Press Secretary is supposed to say whatever they are told to say."

"Well, we both know I've never been very good at that. And I can't, in good conscience, promote someone else's bullshit agenda. The Democratic Party would nominate Hilter's grandson if they thought he had a broad enough election base."

"And you don't think the Republicans are the same way?"

"I think the Republicans are *exactly* the same way. If the Dems put up a minority and a woman, they'll try to find a war hero and a handicapped person to run. It's called counterprogramming, political style."

"So, what are you going to do? Join the Green Party?" Peter asked sarcastically. "You don't even recycle."

"Not the Green Party."

Dan slapped the morning edition of the New

York Times down on the table. "Take a look at page 8."

The Headline read, *Carr Begins Organizing Unified Party.*

"What's that all about?" Peter asked.

"Read it."

Peter began reading aloud, "James Malcolm Carr, the soon-to-be retired President of Pacific National Bank, has begun assembling a committee whose sole responsibility will be to search through nominations to find a candidate to run in next November's Presidential election." He looked up with a cocked eyebrow before he continued, "Carr, a former member of both the Republican and Democratic Parties, is widely credited with keeping the Seattle-based PNB afloat while many of the nation's top banks went under, and is considered a financial wizard. He believes the new party will be able to get their candidate on the ballot in all fifty states."

"Good luck with that," Peter said wryly.

"Yet, he claims to have no interest in running for the highest office in the land himself," he continued. "'We are accepting nominations from any US citizen anywhere, regardless of party affiliation, until we find the most qualified candidate money *can't* buy," Carr announced. Peter smiled. "Catchy slogan."

"He's an extremely bright man with friends on both sides of the aisle," Dan said.

"Some might say *enemies* on both sides."

"Pete, I'd rather lose supporting something Itruly believe in, than win at something I don't."

"Well, I think you're committing career suicide, but I wish you luck my friend if that's the road you want to walk down."

V
~THE ELECTRICIAN'S WIFE~

*B*ernice Kreps worked as an educator ten hours a day, ten months a year for more than 30 years, while her husband, an electrician by trade, worked in education on the side for three hours a day, three months a year. And yet, if you were to ask the average person in the community, most would know of Joe Kreps before his wife. The crazy thing was that Bernice was teaching students to read and write, while Joe was teaching them to win football games. It showed exactly how out of whack the sense of values in most communities were.

It was also the very reason they met. Back in the late '70's, education budgets were tight, and it was a constant battle to get them approved each year. The first cuts were always in personnel. Class sizes grew as teachers were laid off. If that didn't get them under the magic number, they cut out entire programs. As an elementary school English teacher, Bernice Maloney's job was safe. English, especially at that age, was a necessity. But she saw nearly a dozen of her fellow teachers laid off every year, while the athletic department went unscathed. Armed with that information, she took her fight to the school board.

"For the past several years, we've had to endure across the board layoffs," she protested at the monthly meeting of the Board of Education. "And now, you're trying to eliminate an entire program."

"I'm not sure I understand your concern, Miss Maloney," one of the board members responded. "Your department will not be affected."

"I understand that," Bernice said. "But my job as an educator is to educate the whole student. And I don't see how we can do that if we eliminate the Fine Arts program."

"We're faced with difficult decisions all the time. And if we're forced to choose between eliminating English and Math or the Art program, we're going to choose the Art program every time," another board member added.

"Meanwhile, the athletic program has gone untouched," Bernice shot back as the room went silent. She had just touched on the untouchable subject. "The equipment budget for the football team alone would nearly pay the salary of one of the teachers you are laying off. And the football program affects only 75 people in the entire district while the art program has nearly 200 students."

"Let's be honest, Miss Maloney. Most of those students take art as an elective and a relief from their other classes. How many of them are actually going to pursue it as a career or even take a class in college?"

"More than the number of players on

the football team that are going to play in college or the NFL," she answered confidently. The Board Chairman nodded, but it was difficult to tell whether it was a nod of agreement or one that was simply to buy him some time to think of a response. "There's also the financial issue to consider, Miss Maloney. The art program costs thousands of dollars to run each year, while the football program pays for itself. It actually makes money for the district."

"Sometimes you have to spend money to make money," Bernice responded. "If you truly want this school district to be a Blue Ribbon district where the state will award more funding, you need to offer a well rounded program. A winning football team has never made a school into a Blue Ribbon school."

The members of the board finally realized the conversation could continue for hours in this circular motion if they allowed it to. "We appreciate you coming down here tonight and sharing your concerns," the Chairman said at last.

"Translation—thanks for coming, but we've already made up our mind," she answered.

"Miss Maloney, if you can find a way to cut $100,000 from the budget or raise that money, we can keep the art program."

A hand shot up in the back of the room. It was dark back there, and difficult to make out the face. But the voice was deep and would have commanded attention even if it didn't belong to the coach of the high school football team.

"Maybe I can help," Joe Kreps began. "First of all, we can get by with half of our allotted equipment budget. That's 10 grand right there. Then, if we charge seven dollars a ticket for home games instead of five, that will raise another twenty thousand. The concessions bring in $7,500. And then there's my salary. I'll donate it to the cause. That should get us halfway there. If the district can find the other 50 grand, I don't see any reason why we shouldn't be able to keep the art program."

The room was a buzz. "That really isn't necessary," the Chair responded, "although it is a noble offer. Besides, Mr. Kreps, while that may help us with this year, what happens next year, and the year after?"

"Why don't we just worry about this year?" Joe said. "Next year, some rich alum might die and leave the district a million dollars."

Joe Kreps had saved the day and received a hero's congratulations from all in the room. "Thank you," Bernice said once the excitement had died down. "I didn't realize you were a fan of the arts."

"I'm not," he answered. "I just thought you were cute," he added as he left the room.

A week later, they were dating—the town hero and the town crier. Six months after that, he walked into her elementary school classroom wearing a gorilla suit and began pouncing on the chairs and desks as the kids went wild. Dropping to one knee, he held out a ring box in his paw. They were married a year later in an outdoor wedding on the beach. Two months after that, Joe Kreps suffered through his first losing season as a football coach, but he couldn't have cared less. His life was finally complete. Besides, even though he didn't know it at the time, help was on the way. A student who would one day become the greatest athlete in school history entered his wife's 1ˢᵗ grade class that same fall.

VI
~DOCTOR HEAL THYSELF~

*W*illiam Cummings began his lifelong feud with the world on the day he was born. He arrived two weeks and 14 hours later than expected, almost in defiance of a world he knew would be inferior to his intellect. William was the product of a father who died of cancer weeks after he was born, and a mother who then had to work multiple jobs just to keep a roof over their heads. The result was a childhood rich in independence, but bereft of guidance on small, but important things such as how to interact with others.

His mother was an amazing woman, but as was the Catholic way, ridden with guilt over the lack of time she was able to spend with her son. Whatever time she did have, she spent unknowingly nurturing his growing sense of superiority. It was a sense developed more as an instinct of survival than anything. At heart, he was really an insecure boy, craving approval from anyone who would offer it, and if no one was willing to give it, he found the need to give it to himself.

William also fancied himself an athlete, but

was the furthest thing from it. His claim to fame was finishing 3rd in a high school Cross Country race his senior year. In the years that followed, whenever he relayed the story to any poor soul who was trapped into listening, he left out the fact that neither of his school's top two runners ran that day—one due to injury, the other to sickness— and the other three schools in the meet were the weakest schools in the conference, if not the entire state. His letterman's jacket was his most valued possession, and he wore it until the silver leather sleeves were black, and the letters on the chest were falling off.

He had visions of attending nearby Yale after high school, and one day wearing a navy jacket with a bright white "Y" sewn onto the front, but it never quite materialized. William's grades were top notch. He was 3rd in his class. He was also a founding member of the Math and Science Clubs at his high school, and President of the Varsity Club as a senior. The latter was an honor usually bestowed upon the best athlete in the school, which he clearly was not, but the person he was running against withdrew on the day of the election.

Even with all of that in his arsenal, William was still deferred from Yale in the Early Action period. By the time he was accepted in the late summer, the additional scholarships he needed to help with tuition were already gone, and he ended up at the University of Connecticut instead. At UConn, he was known mostly as the strange kid who always wore a long sleeve t-shirt under a short sleeve one no matter what the temperature. When someone asked him why, he responded simply, "Because I can then pull my sleeves over my hands when opening doors. You have no idea the germs that are transmitted on door handles and railings."

When they followed that question with why he wore a short sleeve one over the long sleeve, he answered, "The long sleeve is for a purpose, the short sleeve is for expression."

Strange though he was, there was no denying his academic brilliance. And yet, while he had a mind suited for teaching higher education, he had a personality suited for research. That was where he spent the years immediately following his college graduation. He remained at UConn where he earned his Doctorate in Astrophysics, but amazingly sought out a career as a weatherman instead. It was the oxymoron that was his life. William never appreciated his strengths. In fact, he spent most of his life chasing his weaknesses. If a cute, bright girl who was impressed with his knowledge trailed after him, he failingly chased after cheerleaders instead. And although his scientific mind could have landed him a well-paying job at nearly any research university in the country, he accepted a job at a network television affiliate as a meteorologist who produced forecasts for better looking and more personable people to read on the air. For someone who was such a quick study, he was a slow learner in life. Five years later, he finally was accepted to Yale—this time as a professor.

He was the professor who struggled to teach to large numbers of students at once, but brilliant in a one on one situation; the professor with few friends on the faculty, until something occurred in the atmosphere that they didn't understand.   But mostly, he was the professor who would have rather been an on air weatherman or a professional athlete—even if it was only for a day.

VII
~RIPPING BEN FRANKLIN~

*J*ames Carr learned the value of money when he was only five years old. He had attempted to imitate his older brother's magic trick of pretending to rip a dollar bill in half, but there were two problems. The first was that the only bills he was able to find in his father's wallet had pictures of Ben Franklin on them. The second was that he wasn't very good at the trick.

When his father eventually found the shredded pieces of Ben in the kitchen trashcan, James found himself on lockdown in his bedroom for the next three weeks. "There are three things you need to know in life," his father told him that day. "1) Don't ever play with money. 2) Don't joke about money. and 3) Don't joke about joking about money."

Armed with those three pillars of wisdom, James Carr Sr. made millions of dollars by the time he was 40, as he ascended from bank teller to President of the largest bank in Seattle. James Jr. followed in his footsteps—sort-of—which is to say he too, went to work at the bank, overseeing the Investments & Securities branch and eventually succeeding him as the bank President. But unlike his father, Junior had interests other than work.

Most people make the claim that you'll never meet your wife at a bar, but that's exactly where James Jr. met his; the ironic thing being he wasn't even a big drinker. But his friends convinced him to go out one night so they could introduce him to a girl they knew he would love. It took him all of three seconds—he claimed it was the warmth and softness of her handshake—for him to realize they were right. Maybe it was *because* of that realization that he grew nervous and drank more than he should have. Ten drinks later, on a dare, he ran his hand along the back of her sweater and undid her bra in the middle of the bar. She was so stunned that she couldn't even muster the strength to slap him across the face. Part of her was also secretly impressed that he had been able to do that through three layers of clothing.

James apologized profusely for four weeks straight following that night, and even joked years later after they had long been married, that he was "still paying" for that indiscretion. Of course, he had more than made it up to her over the years. Their home was never short of flowers, and he recognized the importance of cozying up next to her on the couch to watch a horribly sappy movie on the *We* network while a Seahawks game was on the other channel. He also loved her independence. Ellen ran a successful public relations firm that represented most of the television personalities in the area, and James was at every important party or opening she had for one of her clients.

He was an even better father to their two children. James attended every soccer game, play, art show or spelling bee that his son and daughter ever participated in. But his refusal to match the 80 hour work weeks that his brother and father regularly put in left him as the Black Sheep of the family. In fact, his father never appreciated James's "warped sense of values" until many years later when he became sick, and James was the one who took care of him.

"I'm sorry," his father said from a hospital bed on the day he died.

"What are you sorry for, dad?"

"You're a great father and a great son. I'm sorry I didn't realize that sooner."

"Thank you," James said. He didn't know what else to say.

"And I'm sorry I wasn't around more when you were growing up."

"You were around plenty, dad."

"But if I was around more--" he continued. There was a long pause while he gasped for breath. "If I was around more—I might have been able to stop you from tearing up those $100 bills when you were five."

VIII
~HOMELESS AT LAST~

*J*immy Davis had spent most of his brief adult life looking out for himself. He had done it more out of necessity than selfishness. His was the ever increasing and always sad story of an alcoholically-induced, abusive father, and a mother too weak to do anything about it. After enduring years of beatings and broken bones, on the morning of his 16th birthday, Jimmy rose as the early morning South Carolina sunshine began to gleam through his bedroom window. He packed a bag with as many things as he could fit in it, stole a hundred dollars from his old man's wallet, and went over to his high school to officially withdraw.

He did that so no authorities would come looking for him, and he doubted his parents would—his father because he didn't care, and his mother because at least some small part of her, probably did. His big mistake that day was going back to the house one more time before leaving town. He wasn't even sure why he did. Something just drew him back there. When he arrived, he heard his father screaming at his mother. Like an emergency room doctor, he had grown largely immune to it by this point, the difference being, he was now the cause of the rage.

"You stole money from me!" his father's voice echoed throughout the neighborhood.

Hearing it from outside the house for the first time made him wonder why the neighbors never interfered or at least called the police. There was no mistaking the violent undertones.

"I have no idea what you're talking about," his mother pleaded.

"I had a hundred dollars in there last night!"

"Maybe you thought you did? You were pretty drunk." She said it as if they had attended a college frat party.

"You calling me drunk *and* stupid?" he bellowed.

"No..." she said, her voice trailing off.

Jimmy knew what would happen next. Without hesitation, he walked to the garage and pulled a tire iron off the wall. Almost robot-like, he entered through the kitchen and stalked down the hallway.

"You!" his father screamed when he saw him. "You're the one who stole my money!"

Jimmy didn't answer him, and he didn't hesitate. He just swung as hard as he could—years of anger, fright and intimidation fueling the swing—smashing his father flush across the side of his head. His mother screamed as his father crumpled to the floor in a heap, but Jimmy didn't even acknowledge her. He had done it as much for himself as he had for her; probably more for himself, because a large part of him blamed his father and her equally. Him for being a drunk asshole. Her for allowing it to continue. Jimmy didn't know if he had killed him and at that moment, he didn't care. Instead, he stuffed the tire iron in his bag and walked out of the house with no intentions of ever returning.

Less than an hour later, he was on a bus to Danbury, Connecticut, the only bus that left immediately with an empty seat on it. He wasn't sure what he was going to do when he got there. He knew he needed to get a job. He just wasn't sure where. What he didn't realize was that would be more difficult than he thought. Other than fast food restaurants, not many places were in the market for a 16 year old high school drop out. Even the people who worked at the water park had high school diplomas. Some had graduated from college. He eventually settled in as a day shift "sandwich artist" at a Subway in Salisbury for minimum wage. The problem was it took two weeks before he would receive his first paycheck and he had no money left after the bus fare. For the first time in his life, he was homeless, but at least he was safe. He thought about how crazy that statement sounded, but it was true.

He ate every meal at work. He was most likely the only person in the country who had actually tried every different sandwich at Subway. When he got sick of a particular kind, he switched up the bread he ate it on. White, Wheat, Italian Herbs and Cheese. He had tried every combination.

It would take him a month of 60 hour weeks

before he had enough money to rent a room. He spent the first two weeks sleeping outside. He slept underneath freeways, in secluded areas of local parks, occasionally in a homeless shelter. But people always asked questions there, so he opted to keep himself as secluded as possible. He was also scared of what someone might try to do to him in his sleep. Some of the homeless reminded him of his father when they drank—which was pretty much all the time.

No longer in high school, he had become a student of the streets. He watched people in ripped t-shirts and ratty jeans beg for money, then climb into a Mercedes in a back alley. He saw hookers do things in the back of cars, he hadn't seen in the raunchiest of pornos. And he watched as the cleaning crew at a local Catholic high school, spent most of the night shift alternating between playing cards and vacuuming. He watched because that high school is where he eventually slept most evenings. He would wait in the bushes just outside the entrance and when they went inside, he would dart out and slip a small piece of wood in the door to stop it from locking behind them. When he was certain they weren't watching, he would slide inside and follow them on their rounds, sleeping once they had left for the evening. The office he chose was comfortable, if unspectacular. But to someone who had slept in the bushes of Rogers Park, the black leather couch was like a sleeping on a King sized bed with a mattress pad and a thermal blanket. There was even a television in the office.

And yet, in the two weeks that he slept there he had never really bothered to look at the stenciled name on the door. But on the last night, he thought he should at least look at the name of the man whose office had probably saved his life. It read...

Office of Athletics
John Mann, Athletic Director

IX
~THE NOMINATIONS PLEASE~

*N*early a hundred or so people were working the phone lines and sifting through stacks upon stacks of unopened mail in a smallish, but stylish office in the Bellevue area of Seattle. If you wanted to be taken seriously, you needed to at least look the part. Pat Sheehan was in his early forties, and good-looking despite not being much of a dresser. He had James Carr's ear in a corner of the room and pointed to where Dan Holmes was seated.

"What do you know about this guy?" Pat asked.

"His references all check out. Williams grad. Used to work for a big PR firm in Boston. Joined the Democratic National Committee as a speechwriter five years ago. Wrote a good portion of O'Bannon's keynote address at the 2012 convention."

"Then why is he here?"

"Why are any of us?" James asked rhetorically.

"Aren't you worried that he might be a plant to see who we're going to put up?"

"Have I thought about that? Sure. Am I worried about it? Not particularly."

"Why not?"

"Because first of all, if we are truly interested in changing the way things are done, we have to be a little trusting. We said we'd take anyone, regardless of prior party affiliation. And secondly, if we find the right candidate, it won't make a difference what anyone knows or doesn't know," James explained.

"Fair enough," Pat answered.

They joined Dan. James extended his hand. Dan stood and shook it. He looked a bit unsure of himself, but it was difficult to tell if that was because he was intimidated, or worried he was making the wrong decision.

"Welcome aboard," James said before he addressed the entire room, "Listen up, everyone. We have 25 sack loads of nominations to sift through by the end of the day. From them, we need to find twenty candidates worth taking a closer look at." He held up a few pieces of paper. "Some of them, can be discarded rather quickly. For example..." He began to read, "My 22 year old cousin, Vinny..."

He threw the paper in the trashcan.

"You need to be at least 35 to run for President." He held up another one. "My brother Ron, is a card carrying member of the NRA and lifelong anarchist..."

He threw that one into the trash as well.

"Not exactly what we're looking for." He held up a third sheet. "The Priest in my parish loves little boys..."

He grimaced and dropped this sheet as if it was carrying the plague.

"Pretty sure no words are necessary for that."

A man in the corner raised a finger. "I think I've got something, James," he said.

"What have you got, Tommy?"

"A high school football coach and Athletic Director in Connecticut."

"Well, that would be great, if we were organizing a touch football game."

"There's a bit more to it. Apparently, they call this guy The Savior of St. Francis. When he showed up at the school, the enrollment was way down and they were talking about closing the doors after 87 years. So, he cleaned house and brought in a whole new staff of coaches. Then he got the diocese to invest what little money they had available in the athletic facilities, equipment...and so on. Sure enough, they started attracting athletes, some of whom had brothers and sisters and friends who were good students. As the teams started having success, the enrollment numbers kept climbing. He then got the school to reinvest the money into the academic side of things. New science labs, computers, higher salaries for teachers...and now the place is booming—even with the economy."

"Interesting," James nodded.

"This is straight from the nomination letter," Tommy said before he read, "*John Mann is fiscally responsible. He doesn't spend money he doesn't have, and he raises the money he needs.*

He's Catholic, but he's the least judgmental person I know. He's sympathetic, and yet has the forsight to make difficult decisions in the best interest of the school as a whole, knowing full well, that those decisions will be unpopular with some. He's not my type, but I guess he's good-looking. He's personable, well-spoken, and quite simply, the smartest person I know. He's never been married..."

"That right there qualifies him as the smartest person I know," Pat interjected to laughter.

Tommy continued with a smile, *"He has no kids of his own, but is great with them. A role model. A leader. And someone you would want in the trenches with you in a dogfight."*

"Sounds like a good Hallmark Movie. But not sure he's what we're looking for," James said.

"He's not a politician, but could have been a excellent one," Tommy continued. *"In fact, he would be excellent at anything he tried. There's only one problem the way I see it. The goofy bastard wouldn't want the job."*

"Goofy bastard?" Pat asked.

"That's what it says."

"Now *that,* is most interesting," James added.

"Excuse me?" was Tommy's confused response.

"Who in their right mind would want it? I know I wouldn't. Find the person who's willing to do it, even though they don't want to, and that's our person."

"I'm not following you."

"The person who'd be willing to run when

they don't want to, would be doing it for the right reasons."

"There is one more thing you should know about him. You remember that guy about ten years ago that lied his way into four or five different high profile jobs? Played for the Browns. Was a radio DJ. Played in the World Series of Poker."

"Didn't they call him The Chameleon?"

"Correct."

"What about him?"

"This is the same guy."

"Wonderful," James moaned. "So you want to nominate a lying, gambling, flake for President. The Press won't have too much of a field day with him," he said sarcastically.

"He's a Yale grad," Tommy offered.

"That helps a bit."

"He's also the last person to ever beat Alan Huber in an election."

This seemed to spark some renewed interest from James. "When?"

Tommy smiled. "High school. For Student Body President."

You could almost see the wheels turning inside James's mind. "Let's get somebody down there to find out what this guy is all about."

"Who?"

James thought it over for a few seconds before pointing directly at Dan. "Him."

Pat seemed surprised. "Him?"

"Me?" Dan asked, equally surprised.

"Let's face it. Most of us in this room are

either retired with nothing better to do, or, and no offense intended by this, not exactly brimming with career opportunities. Dan is the one person who walked away from a lucrative career for a cause he believes in. Let's see if this guy, this John Mann, turns out to be a man Dan can believe in."

X
˜THE CHAMELEON˜

*L*egend had it that while watching dozens of people angling to get a better view of a photo shoot, Andy Warhol said to photographer Nat Finklestein, "Everyone wants to be famous," to which Finklestein responded, "Yeah, for about 15 minutes, Andy." The implication was that it was not only difficult to sustain fame, but you wouldn't want to even if you could.

That was certainly the case for John Mann, who after soaring into the national spotlight while winning a bet, decided to then drift back into a life of relative obscurity as an athletic director at a high school not far from where he grew up in Connecticut. The bet was a simple one. After watching an old rival get elected Governor, a conversation sprung forward about whether ability or opportunity was the most important ingredient of success. In an effort to find out, the bet had John obtain five different high profile jobs within the span of a year and succeed at each. He could get the jobs by any means necessary—lie, beg, call in favors—but once he had them, it was up to him. They couldn't be jobs that would jeopardize anyone's life. Nothing like an air traffic controller or neurosurgeon. Just jobs that the average person thought they could do if only they were given the chance.

And so he became a high school basketball coach, a radio DJ, an NFL running back, a professional gambler and a Hollywood talent agent. When it was over, he graced the covers of no fewer than ten major magazine publications, with a potential movie deal as well. But he walked away from it all in no small part, because of a girl. When that didn't take, he stayed anyway, because he felt he was needed there. It was pretty much how he had always lived his life; going where he felt he was needed, and it had always served him well.

* * * *

The woman seated on the couch across from John Mann wasn't wearing glasses, but it was apparent once she opened her mouth, that she should have been wearing rose-colored ones.

"I just don't understand," she began, "how my son isn't playing more. He's a senior, and he plays year round, but there are soccer players playing over him."

"Mrs. Wilson," John replied, "Sam's a great kid, but let's look at reality. He played on the JV basketball team as a junior. Occasionally, a player in his situation will go on to have a good senior season, but that's usually the exception, rather than the rule. As for the soccer players, well, they have as much right to play as anyone else. If the coach thinks they're good enough, then he has the right to play them."

"But some of them haven't been on the team for four years."

"Technically, neither has your son. I think you should focus on trying to make it a positive experience for him."

"But how can it be positive if he's not playing?!" she asked.

"That's your job as a parent," John stated. "Sometimes, we can want something so badly that it hurts. And while I can't say for certain because I don't have kids of my own, it probably hurts twice as much if it's your children that are suffering. But the thing is, everyone has strengths and weaknesses. For example, I would love to be a best selling author, but I'm not a talented enough writer. And I never will be. Some kids, no matter how hard they work, will never be great athletes. Your son falls into that category. But I also know that there are other areas in which he excels, where other people struggle. There's an old saying that the key to life isn't so much getting what you want, as it is being content with what you have."

Mrs. Wilson didn't know quite how to respond. She knew anything she said wouldn't come out right. And she also knew deep down, he was right. "Well, thank you for your time," she said as she rose from the couch. "I guess we'll just have to see how it goes."

"I'm sure it will go better than you think. Try not to look at any one game in particular, but look at the season as a whole. Hopefully, at the end, the positives will outweigh the negatives," he said as he opened the door for her.

He found Tom Hubbard waiting on the other side of it. Tom was the gruff, ex-marine, long-time baseball coach at the school.

"Coach Hubbard," John nodded.

"That asshole Kovacs around?" Hubbard asked, barely waiting for Mrs. Wilson to be out of earshot.

"Haven't seen him so far today. What's up?"

"Well, you WILL see him. Apparently, one of the cheerleaders and the Captain of the basketball team were seen doing something they shouldn't have been doing on the bus ride back from the game on Saturday night."

"Making out?"

"Not sure that's what it's called, but it did involve her mouth."

"They did this on the bus?!" John exclaimed. "With everyone around?"

"Apparently."

"Who was it?"

"Shelly Savarese."

John seemed surprised. "Really? She hangs out in here all the time during study hall. She's a nice kid."

"Apparently she is," Hubbard said with a grin.

"I'll look into it. Thanks for the heads-up. Anything else?"

"Don't forget you're having lunch with that guy from ESPN today about the 30 for 30 thing."

"Remind me why they want to do this again?"

"People want to know what happened to The

Chameleon."

"He's a high school athletic director. The end."

"You might want to try to be a bit more interesting than that."

"My life isn't that interesting."

"That was your choice. Other people would have cashed in on their fame."

"I'm doing what I enjoy."

"That's why they want to do the story on you."

John mulled it over. "I'd really prefer they didn't."

"Then tell them that. But only after lunch. I hear the guy's bringing Erin Jones with him."

"I hear she's a little bitchy."

"That's exactly how I like them."

"You're married."

"Like I said," Hubbard smiled. "That's exactly how I like them."

"Easy for you to say when your wife isn't in the room," John laughed.

"I served two tours in Iraq. Do you really think I'm afraid of my wife?"

"I *know* you are."

"Maybe a little," Hubbard laughed.

The intercom buzzed.

"There's a Dan Holmes here to see you," John's secretary said.

"Where's he from?" John asked.

"He says he's from High School Administrator Magazine."

"Is he selling subscriptions?"

"I don't believe so. Something about an

interview."

John shook his head. "Send him in. And have Shelly Savarese come down at the end of the period."

Dan entered the office a few seconds later.

"Dan Holmes," Dan said, extending his arm to shake hands.

"John Mann. "What can I do for you, Dan?"

"I'm from High School Administrator. And we'd like to do a feature story on you and your athletic department."

"Why me? Why us?"

"To highlight the turnaround of the school. At a time when a number of Catholic schools are closing their doors, you guys have had unparalleled success."

"What do you need from me?"

"Just access to you. If it's ok, I'd like to follow you around for a few days. Get a feel for the school and for you."

"I don't know how exciting that will be for you, but be my guest."

"ESPN is coming today to do a 30 for 30 piece on him," Hubbard interjected.

"No kidding?"

"It's obviously a slow week in sports."

"I'll catch up with you guys," Hubbard said. "Let me know when Erin Jones gets here."

"Erin Jones is coming?" Dan asked, intrigued.

"Oh yes."

"She is attractive. Comes off as a little bitchy, but she makes it work for her," Dan added.

"I know, right?"

"If you're that excited about it, why don't you have lunch with her?" John asked.

"Oh, I plan on it. Why the hell do you think I want you to tell me when she's here?" Hubbard answered.

"I'll text you," John laughed.

Hubbard opened the door to leave and almost pulled the man on the other side of it, into the office. Joe Kovacs is exactly how one might picture an academic to look. Tall, thin and not particularly athletic looking, his pants are neatly creased, and his shoes are polished to a shine. He is wearing a navy, v-neck sweater over a button down shirt and tie.

"Tom."

"Joe."

Hubbard left after the icy exchange.

"I know all about it," John said before Kovacs could say a word. "And I'm on it."

"Make sure you are," Kovacs said.

"I will," John promised before Kovacs departed.

"That was just our baseball coach followed by our principal."

"They don't seem to like each other much," Dan answered.

"Yeah, they tolerate each other."

"So, tell me something," Dan began. "I'm sure with your background, you could land a higher paying job at a public school, or even a college. Why do you stay here?"

John thought it over for a minute before responding, and shrugged. "Because they need me."

There was a light knock on his door and a girl stuck her head in. Shelly Savarese was a cheerleader in nearly every stereotypical way. Blond, blue-eyed, and innocently flirtatious, with a body that was perhaps a bit more developed than she was equipped to handle. She was also a bit of a dim bulb. She was on her second go round in at least two core subjects, but she managed to get by because she was savvy enough to manipulate her male teachers and to recognize that she needed to work twice as hard for her female ones.

"Couldn't wait until 4th period, eh?" Shelly exclaimed. "You just had to see me didn't you?" She spotted Dan.   "And who's this? You didn't tell me you had such cute friends."

John turned to Dan. "Could you step outside for a couple of minutes?"

"No problem."

"Oh, Johnny, I knew you'd come around. You want me all to yourself."

"On second thought, why don't you stay?" John said, nervous to be alone with her.

"Any friend of Johnny's, is a friend of mine. I've got nothing to hide."

Dan hesitated at the door, unsure whether to go or stay. John shrugged as if to tell him he might as well stay.

"Grab a seat, Shel."

"Am I in trouble?"

"That depends."

"On what?"

"On if what I heard is true."

"Well, what did you hear?"

"Just that you were seen doing something you shouldn't have been doing with a certain basketball player on the bus back from the game Saturday night."

"We were just making out."

"That's not what I heard."

"What did you hear?!" she exclaimed.

"That you gave a...you know..."

"I know what?"

John turned red and stammered. "A you know what."

"If I knew, I wouldn't be asking."

"What are we, Abbott and Costello? I just heard that maybe you did something not fit for a young lady, and certainly not fit for public viewing."

"That's just a stupid rumor that Mary has been spreading because she's mad at me for making out with Mark."

"Why would she care?"

"Because she likes him."

"Which begs the question of why you would do that if you knew one of your friends liked him?"

"Because he's really cute."

"First of all, even if you only made out, you shouldn't be doing it in public. Secondly, if you're going to do that to one of your friends, you had better be prepared for the consequences and rumors that will follow."

Shelly didn't say anything at first, mainly because she seemed to know he was right. "Am I going to get in trouble?"

"Kovacs has already heard the rumors, so I would do my best to dispel them if I were you. My suggestion is to patch things up with Mary and get the rumor mill shut down. And then sit with the girls in the front of the bus next time."

"Ok," Shelly answered quietly.

"There's an old saying, Shel. Why buy the cow, when you can get the milk for free?"

"What does that even mean?"

"It means, don't give guys what they ask for if you hope to see them again."

"You sound like my father."

"Your father sounds like a wise man."

"No, he's kind of corny, actually. But thanks for looking out for me."

"No problem. And Shelly?"

"Yes?"

"You might want to unroll your skirt before either Father James or Mrs. Harper sees you and gives you a detention."

Shelly smiled. "You think?"

"I think," he nodded.

"I only roll it up when I come in to see you," she winked. "See you later, Johnny."

"I know. I know," John said to Dan once she had left. "She's a real piece of work, but I've always had a soft spot for her," he added, shaking his head.

XI
~THE 29 DEGREE TILT~

*S*cientists from around the globe were in almost unanimous disagreement over the cause of the nation's climate change. Some believed it was the effects of global warming, and while that would certainly explain the soaring temperatures in New England, it did little to explain the four-foot snow drifts in Los Angeles. Others claimed it was a temporary change, not unlike an "Indian Summer". The problem with that theory is that a month and a half hardly seemed temporary, and it didn't explain why Seattle had been left in complete darkness for the past six weeks.

Dr. William Cummings of Yale, had his own theory and everyone was listening. "From what I can tell, the cause of the climate change is the *Obliquity of the Elipse*," he said to a large throng of reporters and a nationally televised audience. "In other words, the tilt of the earth's axis has changed. Over time, it has been somewhere between 21 and 24 degrees. As recently as six months ago, it was measured at 23.27 degrees. This morning, my calculations have it at 29.15 degrees."

"What does that mean?" a reporter asked.

"Basically, it means that the earth has shifted to a higher angle, which means some areas are being exposed to greater warmth, while others are not. As simply as I can put it, because of the shift, in relation to the sun, Los Angeles is now located where Seattle was. Seattle is located where Greenland was. New England is now approximately where the Florida Keys were. And Florida is where Central Mexico was, which also explains why Florida's climate has basically remained unchanged. It also explains why much of the Midwest has remained unaffected by recent events. Being in the center of the country, everything has rotated around it, and it has shifted very little, if at all."

"What caused the tilt?"

"Well, for years now, scientists have believed that only a close encounter with a planet or meteor the size of North America or larger could cause a noticeable shift in the earth's axis or spin rate. It was thought that an encounter like that would probably last at least a week, and the upheavals would horrific. A noticeable change in rotation direction would produce winds with speeds of thousands of miles per hour *everywhere.* Anything not anchored to bedrock would be torn out of the soil and mixed with a world-enveloping hurricane of activity. It was also believed that a direct hit would create earthquakes of magnitudes greater than seven, and even higher. There would most likely be no survivors. But...as you can see, that hasn't happened, so we have to look at other possible causes."

"Have you found any?" a fresh-faced reporter asked, as if he was in Physics class.

"I have a theory," Cummings began, "that a large central air mass in combination with the gravitational pull of the sun, could cause an appreciable tilt in the earth's axis, if the air mass was pushing in the same direction as the sun force was pulling."

And thus, the *Cummings Push-Pull Theory* was born.

"Do you think it will continue?" someone asked.

"I think it's unlikely," he said. "Normally, the air mass pushes in the opposite direction of the sun. They offset each other. I think this is one of those rare occurrences where they worked together. Could it happen again? Sure. But I think it's unlikely to happen anytime soon."

"Do you think it will shift back?" fresh-faced asked.

"I think that's equally unlikely, unless the gravitational pull of the sun drastically changes."

"So you think the climate we have now is likely to stay this way?"

"Keep in mind this is all theory or conjecture on my part," Cummings said. "But yes, for the foreseeable future, I would pack up your snow suits in New England."

* * *

Thirty miles away, John Mann watched the press conference on a small television in the teacher's lounge at St. Francis.

"I went to high school with this guy," John said.

"No shit?" was Hubbard's ever so tactful response.

"No shit."

"He seems like kind of a dork."

"He's actually not a bad guy. Very bright, as you can see. I felt badly in high school because he desperately wanted to go to Yale. We had similar grades and SAT scores, but I scored a few touchdowns my senior year and got in instead of him. They weren't taking two kids from our high school."

"Must have been quite a few touchdowns," Hubbard grinned.

"I guess. But I always felt badly. At least he finally made it to Yale as a professor."

"Here's a question," Dan began, "Do you ever have anything bad to say about anyone?"

"What do you mean?"

"What I mean is that in the brief time I've known you, you've never said anything bad about anyone. Hubbard here is loyal. The principal has his heart in the right place. The cheerleader who gives blow jobs on the bus is misunderstood..."

"*Allegedly* gives blowjobs," John laughed. "And she didn't really give one. That was just girls being girls. I have plenty to say when it's deserved."

"Don't kid yourself. He looks for the good in everyone. He's the exact opposite of me. I don't like most people—especially not that fat tub of shit that's about to enter the lounge."

Brock Ward was a fifty-something History teacher whose ever-expanding waistline was surpassed only by his pompous nature and gaseous emissions at all points of the day.

"Gentlemen," he nodded in acknowledgement of them. "And who is this on the TV?"

"A scientist from Yale who is giving his theory on what caused the weather pattern changes. Apparently, the earth's axis has tilted from its norm of 23 degrees to 29."

"23.27 degrees," he corrected. "I read about it yesterday. Yes, it seems like another catastrophe for our commander-in-chief to screw up. Thank god we only have another year with him."

"Brock, you do realize that both times the President ran he received more votes than your beloved President Clinton. Clinton never received a majority either time. That means that more than half the country didn't want him as President."

"Is that what your extensive athletic department analysis tells you? Did you come up with that while shooting *hoopies*?"

"It's hoops, not hoopies. And I just think you should be more sensitive to other people's viewpoints that are different from your own. I also think you should have a little respect for the office of the President."

"Respect for the man who sent us into war, drove up a huge debt, which in turn plunged us face first into a recession?"

John, silent until this point, entered the

conversation. "Actually, Brock, the economy is cyclical. It would go up or down if you or I were President if it was that time. Recessions are the fallout from greed during times of prosperity. When things are going well, big businesses spend more than they should, and agree to outrageous demands from labor unions because they can't afford a work stoppage. Then business slows, and they pay the price. They end up laying off a number of employees, who in turn stop spending money in small businesses. Mortgage payments are missed. Houses are foreclosed upon. People pull money out of the market in a panic and the Dow crashes. When things bottom out, the economy corrects itself."

"It never bottoms out for the wealthy. Heaven forbid the Republicans actually tax them," Brock maintained bombastically.

The twelve or so other teachers in the room stopped paying attention to the television. In fact, most of them even stopped eating as they listened in on the debate.

"This country was built on capitalism and free-enterprise," John said calmly. "What gives anyone the right to reach into someone else's pocket just because they happen to have a little extra change in there? The rich do pay more taxes. They just shouldn't have to pay a higher percentage of them. What this country needs is a flat tax. Say it was 15%. Someone making $50,000 a year would pay $7,500 in taxes, while someone making $500,000 a year would pay $75,000. I know you're a history teacher, but that's actually $67,500 more in taxes. It's just not a higher proportion, nor should it be. What we also need to do is eliminate the loopholes. What you owe is what you owe. That way the government would have a better idea how much money will be generated from taxes, and therefore, a better idea of how much money they will be able to spend. But maybe you prefer Communism or Socialism? It worked out so well in the Soviet Union."

The room was silent. Hubbard winked at Dan with a smile. A female student opened the door to the lounge. "Coach Mann, Mrs. Peterson asked me to let you know Miss Jones and her producer are waiting for you in your office."

"Thanks, Janice."

Hubbard swept the table clean of food and debris and had it in the trash before John had even slid his chair back.

Erin Jones was tall, smart and beautiful, although not overwhelmingly friendly. She was a former All-American Volleyball player at Duke who had settled into a job at ESPN shortly after graduation. She started covering volleyball and Sportscenter on ESPN News, but had worked her way up to covering college football as a sideline reporter in addition to hosting their documentary pieces and specials. She had made a few enemies along the way, in part for her willingness to stomp on anything in her path to get what she wanted, but also from people who resented her rapid climb, refusing to acknowledge she was more than just a pretty face.

"Thanks for coming down today. This is my Associate Athletic Director, Tom Hubbard," John said upon meeting her.

Hubbard appreciated his effort to make him sound important in front of her. She shook his hand but didn't say anything.

"And this is Dan Holmes. He writes for High School Administrator Magazine and is here doing a story on our school," John added.

"I'm a big fan," Dan said.

"Thanks," she responded flatly.

"So how can I help?"

Erin's producer jumped in. "The way I see it, this isn't so much a *Where is he now?* piece, as much as it is a *Where could he have been?*"

"I'm not following you."

Howard Rozum set the stage with his hands. "What if a man didn't walk away from his 15 minutes of fame? What would he be doing now?"

"Probably sitting in Celebrity Rehab or some other dumb reality show," John answered. "I'm sorry guys, but I'm just not excited about doing this. I try to not ever look back at a decision once I make it."

"Howie, why are we here? No one cares about this guy. Even he doesn't want to do the piece."

"Erin, you were probably too busy picking out prom dresses to remember this, but a little more than ten years ago, this guy was the most famous person in the country. He made the Final Table at the World Series of Poker."

"So have about 1,000 other online geeks."

"He had a popular syndicated radio talk show."

"So does Mike Huckabee."

"And he led the Cleveland Browns to the playoffs."

"The Browns made the playoffs?" she said, surprised. "When was that?"

"Twelve years ago. They haven't made it since. And he was all of these things at the same time. He was The Chameleon."

"And now he works at a dilapidated high school in Connecticut. That makes a lot of sense."

"It made sense to me," John offered.

"If you were so famous, why here? Was it for a girl?" Erin asked.

John didn't respond this time.

"It was!" she exclaimed. "Women do that all the time. But a man...so what happened?"

"It didn't take," John shrugged.

"Then why didn't you leave?"

"I was comfortable here. And maybe I thought the train had left the station. Besides, I had always led a pretty simple life. Didn't see the need for that to change."

"There seems to be more to this story."

"Which is why I want to do this," Howard interjected.

"Ok," she relented. "Why not? I'm game if he is."

Hubbard answered for John. "He is."

XII
~THE BEATEN, THE BROKEN &
THE DAMNED~

*J*oe Kreps rationalized that it must be a female thing. Like his mother before her, his wife had become oddly religious as she grew older. Maybe it was out of fear for her own mortality. Maybe it was because she thought Joe needed all the help she could muster. Whatever the true reason, Bernice Kreps went from a holiday church service attender, to a weekly one—during the holidays, as often as three times a week. That also meant Joe had become religious by default.

He wasn't an atheist. He belonged, as his wife referred to it, to the *Church of Joe*—which meant he believed that it was just as easy to pray from his couch, as it was to drive twenty minutes to do it while kneeling on a wooden pew. Having been raised in the Catholic Church and schools, he had also seen his share of less than friendly nuns and a few alcoholic priests. Joe thought it was far more important to actually *be* a good person, than to apologize afterward for not being one.

The other thing he noticed about his wife was her recent interest in community work. This, he attributed to the free time she now had available after retiring from teaching. Unfortunately, it also meant late nights and early mornings for Joe at the local soup kitchens and homeless shelters, as he didn't want her traveling alone to those areas of town by herself. So he became a good person more by force than by choice.

It was a damp, drizzly night as he followed his wife up the steps of the one-time church that was now a shelter. Normally, the weather would have made him miserable, but it was the first rainfall in weeks, so it was a welcome change. The building the shelter was in, like most of the people inside it, was one good washing away from being beautiful. Joe actually didn't mind going to the shelters. He had always considered himself a student of human nature. He learned about people by studying their expressions, and their reactions in times of trouble. And he had always wondered how someone ended up homeless. Like many people, he thought it was simple. There were plenty of jobs available if you were willing to work hard enough. He had predetermined those that were homeless, were homeless by choice, because they were either too lazy, or too proud to get a job they determined was below their standards. Occasionally, although not very often in his own mind, Joe Kreps was wrong about things.

He settled into the food line, heaping mashed potatoes and gravy onto paper plates as people filed past. He rarely looked up, preferring instead to listen to the conversations around him. There were a few that clearly were battling addictions, whether it be alcohol, drugs or gambling, but without looking up, he had a difficult time telling the difference between the people there and someone he might pass on the street.

"Hi, coach," a voice said as Joe handed a plate to the outstretched hand before him.

He looked up with a start, angry that his wife would have shared details about their private life with strangers. How else would anyone know he was a coach?

The man must have sensed his confusion for he quickly added, "It's Eric Holland."

Joe tried desperately to picture the man before him with a haircut, a shower, and a change of clothes, squinting as if doing that would make the man's beard, mustache and premature wrinkles disappear. It was the eyes that finally did it. Eric had always had a certain glint in his eye, and although it had now been reduced to a glimmer, it was still there.

"Jesus, Holland. How are you?"

The ridiculous words came out before he could stop them.

"I'm ok considering," Eric answered quietly.

"What...um," he stammered, "Bernice, I'm leaving the line for a few minutes," he shouted to his wife as he removed his apron.

"What happened to you?" Joe asked once they were seated at a table off to the side of the room. "Last I heard you were in graduate school at the University of Rochester."

"I graduated and got a job on Wall Street. It

paid pretty well," Eric said. "But I spent the money just as quickly as I made it. I was living above my means, and my parents were no longer around to bail me out. I had about seven hundred dollars in the bank when the market crashed and I lost my job. For a while, I was too proud to take just any job, and I got further into debt with gambling. I had to sell my car and just about everything else I owned to pay it off. Eventually, I tried for any job I could find—fast food, retail, you name it. But most of them wanted high school and college kids. They said I was overqualified. Finally, I landed a job at a Stop & Shop, but it didn't include benefits, so when I got sick and had to have my appendix removed, I got back into debt. I make just enough money to stay in a cheap hotel once or twice a week. I'll crash on friend's couch a couple of times, and I'll stay here a couple of nights. I'm trying to save enough to get a place of my own, but it's tough. They all want first and last month, plus security. I had a hard enough time saving two thousand dollars when I was making a hundred and fifty grand a year, much less twenty."

Rarely was Joe as much at a loss for words as he was at that moment. Eric had been one of his golden boys. He was the quarterback on one of his state championship teams that was content to see others get the glory. He was bright, personable and hard working. Joe never could have seen this coming. Eric came from such a great family. But maybe that was it. His family was no longer around. Both his parents passed on when he was in college, and his older sister had been killed in a car accident a few years back.

"Grab whatever things you have," Joe said at last. "You're coming home with us."

"I can't do that, coach."

"It's not open for discussion," he said before adding, "unless you feel like running sprints."

"I don't think I would last too long," Eric responded sadly.

"Then let's go."

When Joe was a little boy, his mother always said that he had an incredible loyal streak in him. You could tell by this look he got on his face. It was one of fierce determination. The thing was, you never knew what it was that would matter to him. One time, he got every single student in the school to save the job of a music teacher whose program was being cut. He didn't even have him as a teacher. Another time, he fought to have a Rockefeller size tree erected in front of the town hall for Christmas, at a time when the push was to be politically correct and not have any open symbols of religion. When others complained, he pushed to have a giant menorah along with any other symbols from other races and religions right along side it. The setting made the national news for its harmony and acceptance of other people's beliefs. And of course there was the day he saved the art program in the district. He, of course, would claim he only did it to meet his eventual wife, but those that knew him, knew otherwise.

He didn't say a word on the drive home, but Bernice Kreps knew her husband well enough that he didn't have to. The look on his face, the same one his mother used to describe to Bernice before she passed away, was enough to tell her that Joe had found another cause.

XIII
~THE MATCHMAKER~

"*I* told you my life wasn't very exciting," John said as he tossed Dan the sports section in exchange for the front page.

"I imagine it is very rarely quiet," Dan answered.

"Well, there's something to be said about having nice weather all the time as an AD. You never have to cancel anything."

The intercom buzzed. "Nick Lawson is here to see you," his secretary said.

"Send him in."

"Nick, my man. Meet Dan Holmes. What's up?"

"I'm in trouble, bud," Nick said, his voice sounding as troubled as his words.

"What is it? What happened?"

"My indoor soccer place is about to go under."

"People aren't playing soccer in Connecticut?"

"Not indoors when it's 80 degrees outside. We sunk almost a quarter of a million dollars into the start up costs, in addition to having another 800 grand in the building itself. I'm not going to be able to make next month's mortgage for the second straight month, and the bank is going to foreclose on us."

"Can you use the place for something else? Like AAU basketball?"

"It costs money to set up the courts, and I'm tapped out."

"What about leasing it?"

"To whom?" Nick asked.

"I don't know. A business of some sort. How big is the place?"

"75,000 square feet."

"And you're near New Haven, right?"

"Not far. We're in Hamden. Why?"

"Just thinking out loud," John said. "It seems like you have two choices. Either sell off the turf and equipment to buy yourself some time on the mortgage, or rent it out to someone on a short term lease."

"I repeat...who's going to want to do that?"

John nodded his head as he mulled it over. "I think I know of such a man," he said as he picked up the phone and dialed a number.

"Hello?" the voice said.

"Jerry Wentworth," John smiled. "What are you up to? Trolling for high school students for your next teen slasher pic?"

"That idea does have some merit to it," Jerry answered, "But no. Although I might as well since I have nothing else to do."

"Production still shut down?"

"It's been six weeks now because of this damn weather."

"Why don't you find another location to shoot in?" John asked as he winked at Nick. "Weather's perfect in Connecticut."

"By the time we find a place, and pay to move the entire cast and crew, the weather will probably turn back. It would be too costly. So now, all the studios are backed up. Actors can't start new pictures because they haven't finished their current ones. Hollywood has been crippled by Mother Nature," Jerry explained. "No scripts are being bought. No new deals are being made. We are on lockdown."

"That's crazy. What happens if the weather doesn't turn? A guy I went to high school with is a professor at Yale and went on the news a few days ago telling everyone he doesn't think it's going to turn back."

"Find us a good place to shoot cheaply, and we'll move."

"Or you could make a porno. I hear porn pays. And I don't think weather is much a factor when you're shooting in a bedroom."

"I'll take that into consideration," Jerry laughed.

"Listen," John said. "I think I may have a serious solution for you. A clear span warehouse in Connecticut that a friend of mine owns. He's just about to put it on the market. I could get you in there before he does."

"What makes you think this place will work for us?"

"It's 75,000 square feet. It's hollowed out so you could build all the soundstages you like.

There's plenty of parking. It's in an area off the beaten path so there's room for expansion. He might even let you lease it to start, and it's probably the best shot you've got to get a movie made sometime this century," John said.

"I just don't know where we're going to get the workers from?"

"Are you kidding me? People hate Los Angeles. It's crowded, but also spread out. You have to drive everywhere and the traffic is brutal. The only thing keeping them there is the weather and now they don't even have that. People will be leaving by the truckload in a matter of weeks."

"I suppose you're right," Jerry admitted solemnly.

"Is this really Jerry Weinberg? You are all about taking chances. You took a chance when you went to work in the mailroom at EAA. You took a chance when you took the job at the studio. And you'll take a chance on this. You're going to look like a hero. I just can't wait to see the Hollyweirdos mixin it up with the old money from the Gold Coast of Connecticut. The cross dressers meet the country clubbers. It'll be the best thing to happen since the Clampetts arrived in Beverly Hills."

"Talk to him and I'll catch a flight out there within the next couple of days."

John hung up the phone with a smile. "Problem solved."

XIV
~EVERY DOG HAS ITS DAY~

*T*he sad but inconvertible truth was that Kellie Maynard would have seemed much more attractive to men if she didn't have a seven year old boy. But unlike women who tried to hide the fact they had a child until their third or fourth date with a guy, Kellie paraded her son openly, regaling all who would listen with tales of his exploits.

"Timmy was so cold yesterday that he walked around all day with his hands underneath his armpits! He even tried to open the door with the inside of his elbow so he wouldn't touch the metal!" she would exclaim. "Timmy got scared during the thunderstorm last night and crawled into bed with me. It was so cute! Timmy scored his first basket in gym class yesterday! He was soooo excited, he went to the nurse's office and called me right away!"

Most of the workers at *Subway* were high school students who simply rolled their eyes at the stories, but Jimmy Davis found it endearing that a young mother would be so completely oblivious that others found the stories boring and even more so that she seemed so completely unaffected by the sacrifices she had to make beginning when she was only eighteen.

He found it so endearing that he probably would have asked her to marry him at first meeting if he could have afforded to. He had begun working there when he was only 16, and after six years, was being groomed to manage the franchise. He and Kellie became like a good bartending team, tossing horseradish sauce over their shoulders to each other and sliding toasted meatball subs along the countertop. They also argued like a married couple with Kellie complaining that Jimmy was mixing olives into the pickle container, and Jimmy complaining that she always burned the peanut butter cookies.

What weighed heavily on Jimmy was that he felt badly about being named manager. He knew she needed the extra money that came with the promotion—not that he didn't—but he knew she needed it more. Then one afternoon, he overheard a regular customer complaining that his warehouse manager had quit, and Jimmy lobbied for the position. It was an electrical company that sold everything from stovetop bulbs to stadium lights, and before long he became a member of the sales team. His departure opened the door for Kellie to become manager at *Subway*, and their combined incomes made it possible for them to get married—which they did the following fall.

Three years later, he was named a Global Rep and transferred to Seattle. Kellie put in for a transfer as well—which was granted—and life was good in the northwest. But with technological growth came a negative side. Longer lasting light bulbs meant fewer sales and there was only so much you could charge for them. Jimmy was facing a potential layoff, when eternal darkness set in. God worked in mysterious ways. The weather and daylight shift had helped them, but had created so much misery for others.

James Carr rose from his desk at the West Pacific Country Club and shook Jimmy's hand. "Thank you for coming on such short notice," he said. "I'm sure you're a busy man these days."

"That is true," Jimmy answered. "We can't keep anything on the shelves and the factories are having a difficult time keeping up."

"I bet. Why don't we take a walk and I can tell you what I have in mind for this place?"

They stepped out through the terrace doors of the lobby onto the practice putting green out back. The snow had melted a couple of weeks ago, but it remained chilly. Not a damp chilly, but a crisp, dry one.

"This weather, although not ideal, would certainly be good enough to golf in, if we only had light," John lamented.

"Definitely," Jimmy agreed, never having swung a golf club in his life.

"The scientists and meteorologists are all saying in a couple of months, it will be daylight here almost 24 hours a day; which is great, but I doubt our members will want to golf at one in the morning. So here's the problem we face. We have contracts with our members that say if the golf course is closed for more than 75 days over the calendar year, they get a portion of their fee returned. That portion gets larger for every day over 75. We've already been closed for 60 and it's March. So, here's what we'd like to do. We want to light the course. Put up towers along the tree lines and angle them such that one tower could help light two fairways at once. Light the whole damn thing up. That way, we can play as long as there isn't snow on the ground. And if it snows, well, we could set up a cross country trail for people to ski on."

"Light the whole course," Jimmy repeated. "That could get a bit expensive."

"We know that, but no more so than if we have to refund our membership fees because we're closed for six months a year. We're prepared to pay whatever it costs. Have to spend money to make money, my friend."

"I'd have to walk the entire course to see where we could put the towers, before I could come up with a price," Jimmy said.

"Of course. And one more thing. If you can get it done by the end of the month, we'll add 10% to whatever the cost ends up being."

"Holy shit," Jimmy said to himself as he climbed into his car. "This is going to be like a two million dollar deal. Layoff my ass. They're going to make me a vice president!"

"Good afternoon, Doris!" he exclaimed to his secretary at slightly lower than a shout as he returned to his office. "Any calls?"

"Dozens," she answered.

"Just give me the highlights," he said.

"Steve Waller called wondering when his order would be complete. Paul Salay wants a price check on replacement bulbs for their company cafeteria. Your mother called. I didn't know she was still alive..."

"She isn't," Jimmy said dryly.

"You also got calls from six different athletic directors in regards to the proposals you emailed them. One of them was from Connecticut. A guy by the name of John Mann."

After his meeting with Dennis, he had emailed lighting proposals to every high school in the country. With business rolling, he could now offer them never before seen deals. But he never expected the response he was getting.

"What was that last one's name again?"

"John Mann," she repeated. "That name sounds familiar. Want me to get your mother on the phone?"

"Get me John Mann, please."

XV
~ 30 for 30 ~

*E*ric Holland stepped outside and took in the fresh morning air. He didn't notice his old coach in the garage.

"You sleep well?" Joe asked.

"Best night's sleep I've had in years," Eric answered.

"Good."

"You're up early."

"I'm old. That's what old people do. Look, you're welcome to stay here as long as you like. But I'm guessing you'd prefer to have some privacy of your own," Joe said.

"Don't worry coach. I'll be gone tonight."

"That's not what I was getting at. You can stay here. You won't bother us, and it's nice to have the company. But if you'd like a place of your own, I've got a friend who owns a duplex. Half of it is empty. He won't require a security deposit or last month. Just first month. It's not Park Avenue, but it's clean, a decent size, and in a pretty central location. If you want it, it's yours."

Joe held out his car key.   "Why don't you go take a look at it and see if you like it?"

"I don't want to borrow your car.   I'll find my

way over there. But thank you."

"You won't be borrowing it. I'm giving it to you," Joe answered.

"I can't take your car, coach."

"My wife's been screaming at me to get a new car for years. She's not much to look at, but she's dependable and I'm sure she's got another couple of years left in her."

"You better be talking about your car," Bernice interjected from the porch.

"Well, yeah, the car too," Joe smiled.

"Coach. You've done enough. I can't take your car."

"Listen. It's not worth a dime on a trade in, but to you, well, you might be able to get some use out of it. If you don't take it, I might as well smash it to bits and sell it as scrap metal."

"I don't know what to say," Eric responded, tears welling up in his eyes.

"You don't have to say anything," Joe said. "That's the beauty of family. Besides, it's not like I gave you a Porsche or something."

Eric reached out to hug the man not given to public displays of affection, but grasped only air.

"I gotta get going," Joe said as he walked past.

Eric couldn't be sure, but he could have sworn he saw tears in his coach's eyes as he did.

* * * *

The line outside *The Gate* was halfway up the block when John, Hubbard and Dan arrived. "Why the hell did we have to come all the way to New Haven to meet her?" Hubbard complained.

"She said she was doing a story down here and

thought it would be a good place to grab a drink," John shrugged.

"In what world?" Hubbard grumbled.

"We will never get inside," Dan said as they approached the bouncer.

"You might be right," John answered, "but we might as well try."

The doorman looked them over suspiciously as they approached. Each night, they faced a hundred people who tried to talk, sneak or bully their way into the wannabe New York City club. And not allowing it to happen was *how* they managed to stay exclusive.

"Look, quite frankly, I'm no one important," John began. "And I know that letting in three older dudes is not in your job description. But we're supposed to meet Erin Jones here, so it would be really great if you let us in to do that."

The man stared down at him, which was a considerable feat, since John was 6'2". In fact, the silence was awkward enough that the three of them had already begun to walk towards the back of the line when the bouncer unhooked the velvet rope and motioned for them to enter.

"I haven't seen her yet, but go ahead," the man said to John. "I'm a big Browns fan. 2002 was my favorite season."

It was the first time in a long time that John had been correctly recognized. He had what he referred to as generic-face, a chameleon like quality where people recognized him, without knowing exactly why.

"How nice was that?" Dan said when they

were inside.

"I guess that depends on your point of view," Hubbard answered.

They grabbed a table directly across from the VIP section of the club, knowing that it would take divine intervention to get past the bouncer manning *that* rope. The décor of *The Gate* was best described as "plush living room", provided that your living room could hold three or four hundred people. At ten o'clock each night, the velvet curtain was drawn back and the live entertainment began. The place had spring boarded many a start up band as well as provide a safe crash landing for bands on the way down. *Creed, Third Eye Blind, The Smithereens* and *Jesus and Mary Chain* all had graced the stage at various points in their careers.

They had just sat down when a waitress came over wearing a short, form-fitting skirt with an oversized napkin for a top.

"A little past your bedtime, isn't it, fellas?" she joked.

"Of course not," John answered before Hubbard had a chance to say something obnoxious. "We have just as much a right to shake our ass as anyone else here."

"Some people have nicer asses than others," she said coyly. John couldn't tell if she was being flirtatious or not.

"And some people's asses are bigger than others," Hubbard said.

John and Dan flinched the moment the words left his mouth. Everyone had a filter that enabled them to think twice before saying something out-of-line. Hubbard's was broken more often than it wasn't.

"What are you trying to say?" she asked.

"You know what? Some people, like Hubbard here for instance, are just big asses. Ignore him," John said.

"With pleasure," she answered before walking away.

"Smooth," John said as he shook his head.

"Thank you for noticing," Hubbard grinned.

"Look at these women," Dan stated, completely in awe of his surroundings. "It's like being in New York City. It sure isn't Seattle."

"Well, I can tell you this much," Hubbard said, "You won't get many hits if you wait for the ball to hit the bat."

"Yeah. Far better to strike out miserably like Hubbard," John chuckled just as an attractive silhouette approached their table.

"Do I know you?" a woman asked John.

"I doubt it, but you might know this guy," John answered while pointing at Dan. "He's the Pepper guy in the new Dr. Pepper commercials. You know the one. I'm a Pepper, you're a Pepper, he's a Pepper. Everybody's a fucking Pepper."

"I thought that was the old commercial from like the 80's," the woman laughed.

"Well, they're bringing it back. And how would you know anyway? You must have been like zero years old in the eighties."

"I took a Marketing class in college that

focused on television advertising," she answered with a smile.

John nodded, impressed. If they were in Los Angeles, her appearance would have led him to believe she was a waitress waiting for her acting break. Beautifully done make-up. A pretty, knock off Versace dress and low-end shoes from *Nine West*. "And this guy here is a video music director. He's worked with everyone from Jay Z to Fall Out Boy."

"He doesn't look like one."

"Well, he is."

"And what about you?" she asked.

"I'm just a high school football coach," he answered.

"So how you guys know each other then?" she asked.

"He's researching a movie by shadowing me around for a few weeks. Hubbard here will be making his feature film directorial debut on the project."

"Are you some famous coach?"

"Nope. I'm a nobody. I just happen to coach nearby."

He was so smooth with his answers that one would have had to think twice even if they knew the truth.

"Well...I didn't mean to bother you," she said at last, looking for an invitation.

"You're welcome to join us," John said.

"I'm with a couple of friends."

"Even better," he answered.

"I'll bring them over," she said with a smile.

"Now, gentlemen," John remarked once she was out of earshot, "the answers to the next three questions on the test are—a Maserati, a beach house and more money than you can count."

"And what happens when she finds out the real answers to those questions are a Scion, a studio apartment in Seattle and slightly more than minimum wage?" Dan asked.

"Hopefully by that point she'll be too in love with your looks and personality to care," John chuckled. "Just don't let Hubbard speak. I'll be back in a few minutes."

John tip-toed his way near the velvet rope that separated the royalty from the plebeians, trying to see if Erin had arrived before them and made her way up there. From his brief encounter with her, she seemed to have few redeeming qualities, but there was something about her—something he couldn't put his finger on—that drew him to her. It wasn't just her stunning model like beauty or considerable fashion. She managed to show off every curve in her figure while not looking trashy. And if the eyes truly were the window to the soul, hers showed an insecure girl who had received everything she wanted in life, only to find that everything she wanted was a disappointment.

Sure enough, she was not only in the VIP section, but she was in the middle of a heated argument with another of the late 20-something beautiful crowd. John attempted to listen without making it look like he was, but couldn't make out what they were saying. He could only hear the rising sound of angry female voices and saw that the crowd around them had swelled. When one of the bouncers by the rope tapped him on the shoulder, he was certain they were going to ask him to leave the area.

"Are you John?" the hulking giant of a man asked.

"Yes," he responded timidly for a person who made his living as a football coach following a brief stint in the NFL. But this guy was altogether different. John figured he could hit him as hard as he possibly could and the man might not even notice.

"You're here to meet Erin?" the man continued.

"Actually, yes."

"Well, you better get up there before things get really ugly," he said. "She's pretty drunk. Got here a couple of hours ago.   See if you can get her out the back."

"Will do," John responded as he rushed into the fire.

"You are an absolute *slut!*" Erin yelled at the other girl.

John recognized her now that he was next to her. Mercedes James was pretty in a more plastic looking way than Erin. She wasn't an actress. She really wasn't much of anything, except rich—having inherited a fortune from her family's tire sales company.

"And you're a tease," Mercedes shot back.

"Ok, Erin, what do you say we get out of here?" John tried.

She ignored him as if his words had

evaporated the second they left his mouth.

He followed it up with, "Erin, let's go."

"I'm kind of in the middle of something right now," she said, at least acknowledging him this time.

He texted Hubbard to get the car and pull it around back.

Now?! was the response.

YES! he texted quickly.

"Time to go," John continued as a few flashbulbs from cell phone cameras began to go off.

He steered her by her shoulders through the path that the bouncer had cleared.

If it wasn't for the lights, crowd and adrenalin of the situation, Erin might have protested John's decision to push her out the back door. As it was, she clung to him like a lost soul in a desperate attempt to find some form of normalcy in a world that had taken on a life of its own. A minute or so later, Hubbard and Dan screeched down the alley, throwing open the door to the car long enough for them to dive inside, before they all sped off into the darkness—leaving dozens of flashing bulbs behind in the far off distance.

The drive back to Salisbury was done mostly in silence, before John broke it by saying, "I promise you I'm not making a pass at you, but I think it might be best if you stayed at my place tonight. No one will bother you there."

He took it to mean she agreed when she didn't respond.

Wedged in between two other lake cottages

with about a foot and a half to spare on both sides, John's home was comfortable, but a far cry from the luxury Erin was probably accustomed to.

"30 for 30," Hubbard whispered to John as he got out of the car. "What if one of the most desirable, female sportscasters was drunk at your house? Would you bang her?"

"I'm not going to bang her, you ass. I'm not going to touch her."

"You're single and not going to bang a hot, drunk celebrity in your own home with no one else around, and *I'm* an ass?" Hubbard chuckled.

"This is the guest room," John said as he showed Erin the room. "It's got clean sheets on the bed, and there are towels in the bathroom closet, along with toothpaste, a new toothbrush and anything else you might need. Feel free to help yourself to a t-shirt and shorts from the dresser if you want to get more comfortable. I'll be up at 6:45, so if you want to jump in the shower before that, feel free," he said as he headed into his room to get a few hours sleep.

"I'm not a stupid bimbo, you know," were the first words she spoke in more than an hour.

"I never said you were," he answered from the other room.

"You say it without saying it every time you look at me," she said. "I have a degree in Communications from Duke."

"Congratulations."

"You think you know me, but I know you. You probably went to some state school and lived in a frat house where you drank beer and played video games and poker every night."

He smiled to himself as he continued to fold up his clothes and readied himself for the next verbal onslaught.

"And why are you being nice to me? You don't even like me," she continued.

John waited until there were no more sounds coming from the other room before he went to check on her. He found her passed out on top of the covers with the lights still on. She had managed to get her dress off and was wearing one of his t-shirts. He eased off her shoes, and pulled the covers up over her.

"Actually, you're wrong," he said as he turned off the lamp by the bed. "For some reason, I seem to like you very much."

She watched him leave the room with one eye open, and the thought occurred to her that maybe, just maybe, she had been wrong about him after all.

XVI
~A REUNION OF SORTS~

"*A*nd you said your life wasn't that interesting," Dan said as he thrust the front page of the entertainment section into John's chest.

On it was a picture with the headline, *Erin Jones' Guardian Angel.* The picture was of John from behind as he shoved her out of the club.

"At least they're showing my best feature," John smiled good-naturedly. "I doubt anyone will be able to identify me from my broad shoulders and my firm, perfectly shaped ass."

"So what happened after we dropped you off?"

"Nothing happened," Hubbard said as he barged into the office.

"What makes you so sure?" Dan asked.

"Because this guy is like a boy scout. Pathetic really when you think about it."

"It is somewhat pathetic," Dan agreed.

"Sorry to disappoint but yes, nothing happened," John assured them. "And not that we don't enjoy your company, but how long are you sticking around here? Bad enough I have to deal with Hubbard. Eh tu, Brute?"

"Well, I was thinking of leaving this afternoon, but I see this invitation here and think it might be worth sticking around for."

Dear John,

We hope this winter finds you in good health. As you are probably aware, due to a generous donation from Emile Whitbeck, Milford High School will be opening a state-of the-art athletic facility, complete with two basketball courts and an Olympic size pool. Also included will be a 100 foot by 100 foot room to honor past athletes and coaches. Our Hall of Fame will open its doors the night of the basketball state tournament's opening round and we would like to commemorate the evening by honoring two of Milford High's greats—yourself and recently retired football coach, Joe Kreps. We would be honored if you could attend the ceremony on Wednesday evening, March 7th at 7:30pm.

Please RSVP to Mary Walsh at (203) 283-4900, extension 93 at your earliest convenience.

"Where is Milford?" Dan asked.
"About an hour from here."
"You going, Hubbard?"
"Wouldn't miss it."
"Then I guess I'm staying."
"Wonderful," John groaned as his intercom buzzed.
"Jerry Weinberg and Jimmy Davis are here

to see you," his secretary said.

"Send 'em in," John said, rising out of his chair. "Gentlemen. I'd like you to meet the most powerful man in Hollywood, Jerry Wentworth. Who, I should add, I knocked out of the final table at the World Series of Poker's Main Event."

"Fucking guy. It's been 12 years. Sing a new song."

"And with him is the most popular man in the Pacific Northwest, Jimmy Davis."

As they all shook hands, Jimmy looked around the unchanged room with equal parts nostalgia and trepidation.

"Jerry is looking to open a movie studio right here in Connecticut, and Jimmy is going to help him light it. He's a Global Rep for Electrical Wholesalers. I appreciate you getting out here so soon."

"Don't thank him. Thank me," Jerry grumbled. "I picked him up in my jet. Seattle isn't exactly on the way to New York from Los Angeles."

"Well, you do stand to benefit from it," John laughed as he looked at the clock. "We should get going. Nick is meeting us there. Hubbard. Dan. You guys want to tag along?"

"Definitely."

* * * *

"So this is it," Nick Lawson said with a grand gesture to the group. "What do you think?"

The hulking metal structure was spacious enough although hardly lavish. Like a person trying to imagine an empty apartment with the furniture in it, Jerry tried to envision it as the new home of Sunshine Valley Pictures.

He didn't say anything at first. He merely nodded his head in thought, before answering, "We could probably fit six sound stages in here."

"I would think at least that many," John added.

"How much of the surrounding land do you own?" Jerry asked.

"Three more acres out back, plus the property next door is for sale."

"It'll be expensive to set up. But it's got definite possibilities. What kind of rent are you looking for?"

"That's negotiable. I've got to be able to pay my mortgage and make a little on top of that."

"Only problem is by the time we set everything up and get everyone over here, the weather will probably be nice again in L.A."

"Yeah, until November. And then you're back to square one. You've got to look at the big picture," John said.

"What happens if the weather turns back?"

"That's the beauty of leasing, my friend."

Jerry nodded again, seemingly convinced. "Can you light this thing up, Jimmy?"

"I could light up a desert for the right price," he answered.

"That's what I'm afraid of," Jerry smirked. "Tell you what. I'll give you a quarter of a million a year for two years," he said to Nick.

"You'd need at least three years to make it worth your while, wouldn't you?" John asked.

"Jesus, Mann. You should work for the government. They like to fleece people out of their money too."

"I'm not making a penny off this," he laughed. "Just trying to help out two friends."

"Fine. Three years. With an option to buy after that."

"Sounds like you've got yourself a movie studio," Nick said, shaking his hand.

"You know any good realtors?" Jerry asked. "I've got to find a place to live. If I don't babysit these morons while they're building it, it will never get done."

"Ok, can we now head to Milford to watch our boy get inducted into the Hall of Fame?" Hubbard asked.

"Are you excited?!" Nick said as he grabbed him around the shoulders and shook him.

"It'll be good to see Coach, again, don't you think?" John answered.

He had always done such a deft job at deflecting praise, that even his closest friends sometimes had a difficult time determining whether he really was that modest, or if it was all an act. His actions over the years, however, certainly told the story of a man more interested in family and friendship, than fame and fortune.

XVII
~THE ECHOES OF CHEERS~

*O*ne man stood near mid-court, not known as much of a public speaker, and yet, he found himself completely unaffected by the surroundings, more because he didn't care than because he was comfortable. The other man, polished and spit-shined on the outside, stood next to him as nervous as he could be. It didn't seem to matter how many times he had spoken in public before. Doing so always left his stomach in knots.

"Thank you all for coming tonight," the Athletic Director began. "It should be a terrific game as our boys begin their quest for the school's first basketball state championship in 17 years. But before we get to the game, we wanted to take a moment to celebrate the opening of the Milford High School Hall of Fame, which you can look into through the windows at the far side of the court. The room was made possible by a generous donation from the Whitbeck Foundation, and tonight we will be honoring its first two inductees. The first is a legendary football coach, who retired last fall after 43 years as our head coach. He is 3rd all-time in the state of Connecticut in wins with 343, and 1st in win percentage, having won an astronomical 84% of his games. He won 7 state championships, including an incredible stretch of four in a row, and 14 conference titles. Over the years, he produced three All-Americans—one of whom is here tonight—27 All-New England, 73 All State and 104 Academic All State players. If you were to ask him, I'm sure he would be most proud of that last number.

And yet, as wonderful a career he had on the field, Joe Kreps might just be best known for saving the fine arts program in the district back in the late 70's. That program has since flourished and is one of the reasons our high school has been a blue ribbon school for the past eleven years. Joe would tell you that he only did it to impress the woman who has now been his wife of 41 years, but the rest of us know better. It is with great pleasure that I introduce the first inductee into our Hall of Fame—Mr. Joseph Kreps."

Joe slowly made his way to the podium careful to take in the atmosphere that included all of his children and grandchildren. He hadn't really thought too much about what he was going to say until that moment. Pausing to clear his throat and collect his thoughts, he began, "I've heard it said that a man is only as good as the woman who puts up with him. If that's true, I must consider myself the greatest man on the face of the earth. Either that, or the luckiest. My wife put up with more than 40 years of late nights watching film and scouting games. She put up with silent nights when we lost, and gave up endless vacation opportunities just so I could be around a game where the object was to carry a funny shaped, leather object into a certain area of an open field. In fact, I would have to live to be 111 just to pay her back for all of the sacrifices she made over the years. She did it because she knew how passionate I was about the game. There was just something about waking up on a crisp, clear Saturday knowing that in a few hours the smell of hot dogs and hamburgers from the grill of the concession stand would be in the air as I led the team out onto the field. To me, it was never about winning. It was about competing. It was about getting the most out of what you had to work with. I remember a parent coming up to me after my first losing season saying, '*A dog has never won the Kentucky Derby, my friend. You did the best you could with what you had.*' And he was right. It was a successful season. I just didn't think so at the time. When I look back years from now, I'm sure I'll remember the state titles, but more than that, I'll remember the boys that I coached, the coaches that I worked with, and the life-long friends that I made. I thank you for this honor, although I'm somewhat embarrassed to be honored for simply doing something I loved. Thank you anyway."

The thunderous ovation grew louder with each passing moment to the point where the usually unflappable coach was visibly touched. He took his seat next to his wife and family, a rare smile on his face, content not just with the evening, but even more importantly, with his life.

"Our second inductee tonight," Athletic Director D'Ambrisi continued, "is one of three All-Americans that played for Joe Kreps. What separates this person from the others is that he was an All-American in basketball as well as an All-State baseball player. On the football field, he holds the state records for most yards gained in a season and a career, as well as most touchdowns scored. In his four years at Milford, he lost just one game, going 51-1 during that span. The football team won the state championship all four seasons he played, a feat that is unlikely to ever be matched. On the basketball court, he led the team in scoring, rebounds and assists all four years, and is the all-time leading scorer with 1,725 points. He led the team into the state final in both his junior and senior years, winning the title as a senior. He was the person with a hundred nicknames. Lightning in bottle. The Shadow— because you could see him, but couldn't touch him. And of course, The Greatest Mann in the World. Those that know him were probably not surprised when years later, he passed up a life as a celebrity to be the Athletic Director and football coach at a high school in Connecticut. It is with great pleasure that we welcome him back here tonight. Ladies and gentlemen, John Mann."

After waiting out the ovation for the better part of a minute, he finally began to speak over the remnants of applause. "Standing here at the podium, I am reminded of the line, 'It's the loneliest feeling in the world; to find yourself standing up, when everyone else is sitting down.' I'm not sure if Mrs. Hodgeman is here tonight, but if she is, I'm sure she'll be impressed that I remembered my *Inherit the Wind*. It's funny. Time has a way of fading even some of our most cherished memories to the point where it is often difficult to determine whether they ever really happened at all, or are more the product of a vivid imagination that remembers things as we want to remember them. I'll be honest with you. I don't remember many touchdowns or big plays I was involved with. I do, however, remember a few of the embarrassing ones. Like when I slipped charging in for a fly ball in center field. The ball caromed so hard off my chest it rolled all the way to second base and we got the guy out trying to stretch a single into a double. I remember heaving in a three quarter court shot at the halftime buzzer and sprinting towards the locker room, only to hear my father shout out, *"Yeah, but you can't make a free throw!"*

I remember Brian Roberts—our hulking defensive lineman—scooping up a fumble and rumbling 45 yards for a touchdown, carrying three people on his back the last fifteen yards into the end zone. One of those people was me, having jumped on in all the excitement.

I also remember that Eric Holland was so superstitious that he refused to wash his socks or his pads until we lost a game, which as you just heard, happened only once in four years.

I remember the time as a freshman when

Coach kicked in the door to the locker room before a game in an effort to motivate us. Our eyes almost popped out of our heads when the huge steel door came sliding across the concrete floor. We didn't find out until years later that Coach had already taken the hinges out of it before kicking it in.

I remember the pasta parties Mrs. Coach used to throw for us in the school cafe the night before games, and the bus rides home after games.

I remember that my parents attended every event I ever participated in. My father even passed up tickets to Notre Dame's last National Championship game back in 1989 so he could watch me play in a high school basketball game.

Those are the things I remember, because those are the things that are important. Not whether you won or lost. It's just easy to forget that from time to time, but I think it's a lesson I learned from each of the coaches I had here at Milford. Along that line, I cannot tell you how honored I am to be mentioned in the same sentence as Coach Kreps, much less honored on the same night. Coach Kreps, along with Coach D'Ambrisi and Coach Powers made me into the athlete I was back then, and helped shaped me into the person I am today. I only hope that the latter is good enough. Thank you from the bottom of my heart for tonight."

The rousing applause died down slowly, but the echoes of cheers in his head would last much longer. Applause wasn't something he heard much of these days. No one ever cheered or gave him an award when a bus arrived on time to take a team to a game. Such was the thankless job of a high school athletic director.

The Hall of Fame room itself was beautifully done. Glass entrance doors and cases holding memorabilia and trophies from nearly a hundred years of teams. The far wall hosted the plaques and bronzed busts of the first two inductees.

"Did they have one of the Special Ed students make these busts?" Joe Kreps said loud enough to embarrass his wife. "It looks nothing like me."

"Looks like Michelangelo himself sculpted it to me," John said. "It captures your surliness perfectly."

"No one likes a smart ass, Mann," Joe responded.

"Except for another smart ass," Eric interjected. "By the way, Mann, thanks so much for letting the entire community know that I never washed my socks or my pads."

"Eric Holland," John smiled. "Figured it was the least I could do after suffering in the locker next to yours for four years. How are you, buddy? Last I heard, you were a big mucky muck down on Wall Street."

"Not so much anymore," Eric answered solemnly. "Had a string of bad luck—mostly brought on by myself mind you—but...I lost my job...and my house...."

"I had no idea. Anything I can do to help?"

"I appreciate the offer, but Coach and Mrs. Coach have been helping me get back on my feet. They pulled me out of a homeless shelter."

"You know," John began, searching for the right words, "this is going to sound trite, and I really don't mean for it to, but when the weather turned, the first people I thought about were the homeless. Obviously, there are homeless everywhere, but I think the greatest number live in Los Angeles, mainly because the weather is usually nice. And then the weather changed, and well..."

"I know," Eric said. "It's difficult. People don't realize how difficult it is. They just assume the homeless are lazy drunks who should just go out and get a job like everyone else. First of all, you have to find a job. Then if you do find one, it takes a few weeks before you get a paycheck. Then even longer to save any money. Most apartments require first, last and a security deposit. That's not easy to come up with. It takes time."

"I know. I mean, I volunteer periodically at a shelter, but I wish I could do more."

"Do more what?" Will Cummings asked as he walked up.

"More to help the homeless," John responded.

"They need to help themselves first," Will answered. "My mother worked two and three jobs to keep a roof over our heads."

"It's not as easy as all that," John said in an effort to quell what was certain to become an uncomfortable situation.

"Will's right," Eric said. "I have no one to blame for my problems but myself. But there are others who didn't have the advantages I had."

"I'm sorry," Will said. "I had no idea."

"It's ok. You're right to a certain extent."

"So..." John broke the silence that followed, "What do you say we move this down to Shabeen's for some wings?"

"I'd love to, but I don't eat and drink with Cross Country runners," Joe said, only half-kidding.

"I was a four year letter winner and President of the Varsity Club," Will said, in an effort to defend himself.

"Thanks to Mann pulling out of the election," the grizzled coach responded.

"He would have won anyway," John said, even though no one really believed him.

"Joe, be nice," Mrs. Coach chided.

"I'm only kidding, Cummings. I'd love to go, but our grandchildren are coming over."

"I've got to get up early tomorrow," Eric said.

"How about it, Will?"

"I'm in," Will said, "as long as you don't mind drinking with a cross country runner."

"I think I could handle it," John laughed.

"I'm not sure I can," Hubbard grumbled as the others stifled their laughter.

Stepping through the front door of Shabeen's Bar was like stepping into a time warp that took you straight to 1990. Pearl Jam played out of the jukebox. The mostly wood bar had stains on it that were older than some of the patrons, who varied in age from early twenties to early fifties.

The only thing new was an outdoor patio deck with five or six picnic style tables. They settled in at one of the tables with a pitcher of Sam Adams while they waited for their hot wings.

"I feel badly about what I said to Eric," Will began. "I really had no idea."

"I know. Neither did I. I think he understood."

"I'd like to make it up to him somehow."

"I'm working on a way to do that," John said.

"Let me know how I can help."

"Once I work out the details, I definitely will."

There was a long pause in the conversation. It was obvious that Will had something on his mind and was simply trying to figure out a way to ask it. He had never been known for being delicate.

"There's something I promised myself I would ask you if I ever had the opportunity," he said at last.

"And what's that?"

"It's a question I'm sure you've been asked a thousand times in the last ten years. How'd you walk away from it all?"

"From what all?" John answered. He knew what he was referring to, but didn't want to seem presumptuous.

"From being a celebrity," Will said.

"I wasn't a celebrity."

"You were on the cover of *Time, Newsweek, People, Entertainment* Weekly and *Sports Illustrated* for cryin out loud! Most people go their entire lives without their classmates remembering their name."

"I was just some guy who won a bet. It wasn't real."

"But out of all the opportunities you had, you decided to be a high school Athletic Director?"

"If I hadn't, I'd have missed out on stimulating conversation with this guy," John said, pointing to Hubbard.

"Blow it out your ass, Mann," Hubbard grinned.

"See what I mean?"

"But don't you miss it? The money? The parties? Hanging out with the celebrities?"

"Meeting celebrities was cool—for about five minutes—until I realized they were just as full of shit as anyone else. Probably even more so. Here's the thing. I'm glad I did it. It was a great experience. But if I never took that bet, it's not like I would have had some huge void in my life. Now, if I never got to teach or coach, *that* I would have missed. As a teacher, I'm sure you can understand that."

"I'm a *professor* actually. A *doctor* technically."

"Excuse me, Dr. Cummings," John laughed.

"This goofy bastard is a doctor? No shock there," Hubbard muttered.

"You know there's something I've always wanted to ask you," John said.

"Ok."

"How come you've never been satisfied with your life?"

"What do you mean?"

"You're always searching for something

better."

"Isn't everyone?"

"When we were in high school, you were a good cross country runner, but you always wanted to be on the football team. You had a lot of cute girls who liked you, but you wanted to date the Captain of the Cheerleading Squad. For college, you were accepted to the Honors Program at the University of Connecticut, but you wanted to go to Yale."

"Who wouldn't?"

"And then you finally got to Yale as a professor, but I get the feeling you'd rather be a television weatherman."

"What's your point?"

"My point is this," John began, "I think it was Malcolm Forbes who once said, "Too many people overvalue what they are not, and undervalue what they are."

"That's easy to say coming from someone who has had everything I wanted," Will answered. "*You* were a football star. *You* dated the captain of the cheerleading squad. *You* went to Yale. *You* became a national celebrity. And you walked away from it all. Do you have any idea how crazy that makes me?"

"I never asked for any of it," John responded.

"That's just it. I know you didn't. And you never rubbed it anyone's face. So many times I wanted to hate your guts, but you made it nearly impossible to do."

"I hate his guts," Hubbard said.

"Me too," Nick added.

"Seriously. He's always been so even-keeled. So modest. It annoys the shit out of me to be honest," Will said.

John laughed. "I'll let you in on a little secret. It's easy to be modest when everyone else is cheering your name. Let's see how I am when the cheering stops for good."

"John, the cheering never stops for guys like you. People probably applaud when you come out of the bathroom."

"Maybe if I've eaten nachos," he replied without missing a beat.

Silent until this point of the conversation, Dan leaned in and said, "*I count him braver who overcomes his desires, than him who overcomes his enemies, for the hardest victory is victory over thyself.* Aristotle."

XVIII
~THE CONFIRMATION~

*A*s he spoke on the phone, John leaned back in his chair, resting his feet comfortably on the desk.

"Nick. It's John. I've got a question for you. With the income from Jerry, are you still planning on refurbishing that property in New Haven down by Yale?"

"Thinking about it."

"When will it be ready?"

"Probably November if I start it soon."

"OK. And how many units are in there?"

"25 singles and 25 two bedrooms," was the answer.

"And what are you asking for each?"

"$800 for the singles and $1400 for the two bedrooms. What's on your mind?"

John scribbled it down on a pad and punched in some numbers on a calculator. "So that comes to a little more than seven hundred grand for the year for the whole building, including a security deposit for each. Here's the reason I'm asking," he continued.

"I can't stop thinking about Eric. I've wanted

to do something more to help the homeless than slopping some soup in a bread bowl. My idea is to provide rent-free housing for a group of homeless people for one year to see if they can get themselves back on their feet. I'll pay the rent for a year. I just need to find someone with a building who is willing to do it. Obviously, it's a risk. There is no guarantee of recouping any damages that might occur, and if they can't pay after a year, it might be difficult getting them out of the building. But if it works, it could be the one worthwhile thing we ever do with our lives."

"How are you going to raise the money?" Nick asked.

"I have no idea," John laughed. "But do me a favor and don't start leasing out the apartments in that building without speaking to me first. I'll get back to you in a couple of days. Thanks, bud."

Dan walked into his office just as he hung up the phone. "You know I couldn't help but overhear part of your conversation. You're doing a project to help the homeless?"

"Trying to. Once the weather turned bad out here, I had this idea that I would round up a group of people that were living on the streets and provide them with transportation to a warmer climate. Now that I know about Eric, I'm even more motivated. But I'm not sure the people of Connecticut would take too kindly to me dropping off 100 homeless people on their steps with nowhere for them to go."

"You're probably right about that," Dan said. "So now I'm trying to find housing for them, which is where Nick comes in. But there is the little issue of being able to pay for it all."

"You need seven hundred grand?"

"Somewhere around that. You have that under your mattress?"

"My mattress is flat unfortunately, but I know of someone that might."

"Well, if you can pull that one off, you'd be a veritable Santa Claus, my friend."

"I'll make some calls."

"So this is it, huh?" John said. "You're finally leaving us."

"Yup. Have to get back to the darkness of the great Northwest. But I have a feeling we'll be seeing each other again," Dan responded.

"Until then," John said as he pulled him in for a shoulder bump.

* * * *

An hour getting through security at JFK, a six-hour flight, forty minutes waiting at baggage claim, followed by thirty minutes in a cab, and Dan Holmes finally found himself walking through the doors of the Unified Party's conference room. Nine people were already in the room with one vacant chair—the one next to James Carr.

"Mr. Holmes. Nice of you to join us," James said in a tone that was more welcoming than admonishing. "We were beginning to wonder if you were coming back!"

"I'm back," he said with a grin.

"With good news I hope."

"I think so."

"Good. Well, we will save you for last then.

Gary. What do you have for us?"

"Walter Jennings. He's a Professor of Economics at Georgetown. As you can imagine, he understands the economy as well as anyone, and as a professor, has the ability to explain it to people in simple terms. Nice enough guy, but...he's a bit Magooish, and I'm not sure how that would play with the voters."

"Interesting," James said. "Tim?"

"Paul Harrington. He's the CEO of Beds and Baths. Extremely bright and personable. Knows how to run a business, and has the ability to negotiate which would be an asset in foreign affairs, but he's got a bit of a temper when things don't go his way. I have a feeling the press would eat him alive."

"What are his political leanings?" James asked.

"Left of center, but even Democrats don't seem to like him much."

"Ok. Barb? What about you?"

"Jane Kassidy is the President of the Make-a-Wish Foundation. Went to Stanford. Runs a multi-million dollar charity that is regularly on the top charity lists. They bring in more than $250 million a year and more than 70% of the funds go to their cause. Her salary is only $130,000 a year, which is well below the Presidents of most charities of a similar size. She's well-spoken, kind and tough when she needs to be. Critics will argue that the foundation is not money well spent. That the money would be better spent on medical research. It could end up creating a national debate on the validity of the foundation, but those that know Jane, *love* her. I could see her slowly gaining traction with voters. The more she got in front of them, the more they would like her and support her."

"Thanks, Barb. Sounds like a very viable candidate. Pete?"

"Jeff Westwood. The actor. More recently known as a director and producer who has won 3 Academy Awards. Very popular among people young and old. Stays out of the spotlight and always has. Spends very little time in LA. Has dabbled in politics as the Mayor of the small Northern California town where he calls home for much of the year. By all accounts, did a great job there. Balanced the budget. Increased town offerings. He was extremely popular. Has name recognition and could probably raise a heckuva lot of money to campaign with."

"What are his negatives?"

"Viewed by some as too liberal and quite frankly, some people want actors to act. They have no interest in hearing the slanted political views of someone who hasn't lived in reality for years and doesn't need to deal with everyday problems."

"Could he win?"

"He'd probably have the best chance of any of our candidates on name recognition alone."

James nodded. "Let's see what Dan has for us."

Dan stood up and cleared his throat. "John Mann is a high school athletic director at a small school in Connecticut. How does that make him qualified to run for President? It doesn't. But he's much more than that. This is a Yale educated guy who can speak on a variety of topics eloquently. He understands how the economy works. He's well-spoken and I could see him on the campaign trail winning over thousands upon thousands of voters every day. The people that work with him and his friends are fiercely loyal. I didn't hear a bad word about him and I was with him for a week."

"That's great. He seems like a terrific guy. But a President?" Pat Sheehan asked. "I just don't see it. He works at a high school for god's sake. The press will laugh at us."

"Here's the thing. We have an Economics professor who's boring. An ill-tempered CEO who pisses people off. The President of a charitable foundation that is criticized for its very cause. And an actor. John Mann majored in Economics at Yale. Everyone likes him. He's currently working on a project to house the homeless who are struggling with the weather pattern shift. Of his own volition. He has name recognition. This guy is the Chameleon. Some of you might view that as a negative, but we could turn it into a positive. He's already proven he could do just about anything. And he's also the last person to beat Alan Huber in an election. Think of how that would play out. It would virtually give him instant credibility. He combines the best qualities and assets of our other candidates all rolled into one. You guys sent me to Connecticut to see if John Mann was a person I could believe in. Well, I believe in him and I would follow him. And so would others."

The room was silent for a few moments after Dan's impassioned plea. It was hard to tell which way people were leaning.

James finally broke the silence. "Thanks, Dan. I'm impressed by all of the candidates. I think we have the ability to make history and make some noise on the national scene. We just have to figure out which candidate to put forth and then decide if any of them would be willing to accept the number two position on the ticket. As we discussed, in an effort to remain unbiased, Sean, Terry, Linda, Pat and myself will be the only ones to vote. In case of a tie, we will eliminate the one not in the tie and vote again. I really want to thank each of you that went to visit with these people for your dedication and for sharing our passion. Sean?"

"Jane Kassidy," Sean replied.

"Terry?"

"John Mann."

"Linda?"

"Jane Kassidy."

"Pat?"

"Jeff Westwood," he answered.

"And I vote for John Mann," James said to the surprise of most in the room. "So that eliminates Jeff Westwood. Re-vote between Jane Kassidy and John Mann."

"Sean?"

"Jane."

"Terry?"

"John Mann."

"Linda?"

"Jane."

"My vote remains the same, so I guess it all comes down to Pat. What say you, Pat?"

Dan hung his head. He knew where the vote was headed.

Pat sat silently for a few moments, chewing on his lower lip in deep thought. "I realize that the likelihood of winning this election is slim to none. But if we are going to be a viable option going forward and change the existing political landscape, we need someone who can at least contend, which is why I voted for Jeff Westwood. And every logical form of reasoning in my body tells me that John Mann can't win. At the same time, we also need to put forward someone to energize this country in a way not seen in a long time. So if this *chameleon* can inspire people the way he appears to have inspired Dan, then just maybe we have something. I vote for John Mann."

Dan was so expecting the vote to go the other way, that he didn't understand why everyone was congratulating him and patting him on the back.

"Well, Mr. Holmes," James said with a smile, "If the nomination letter was correct, the hard part of your job is about to begin. You've now got to convince this guy to run."

XIX
~WHEN IT RAINS, IT POURS~

*T*here was a knock at the front door. It was 9:00am and John couldn't imagine who for the life of him would come calling at that hour. The knocking only grew louder and more repetitive with each passing moment. He made his way over to it and found none other than his old coach, Joe Kreps.

"Hi Coach. What's up?" he asked, looking puzzled.

"I've been trying to reach you all morning."

"Umm, it's only nine o'clock."

"You didn't answer your phone."

"I forgot to charge my cell last night and it died. Everything ok?"

"Everything's fine," Joe said gruffly. "I just thought you'd want to know that Rocco Gerardi retired from Yale."

"No kidding. What was he there for? 30? 35 years?"

"33."

"And you came all the way over here just to tell me that?"

"They've begun a nationwide search for a new

coach."

"I'm sure they'll get quite a few applicants," John remarked casually. "You interested?"

"I'm retired, Mann. They want you. The AD and I go way back. He asked me to get in touch with you."

"Me? Why me? I'm just a high school coach. No offense," he said when he remembered that's exactly what Joe had been for forty years. "But you know what I mean. They'll probably have coaches apply that have NFL experience."

"Maybe it's because you're an alum. Maybe it's because you're one of the only alums who isn't a doctor, lawyer or banker. No offense," Joe responded with a grin. "Maybe it's because you're the only living All-American they have. I have no idea. I just know they want you to meet with them."

"So you're saying they want me because I'm the only alum who's not successful, is still involved in football, who's not dead," John laughed.

"Those last two are important qualities to have, Mann."

"I don't know, Coach. I'm pretty happy where I am."

"Don't be an idiot. When the top academic school in the country with a Division I athletic program offers you a job, you take it. Especially when it's in the area you grew up in and your alma mater. You need Hubbard to knock some sense into you."

It was the sort of no-nonsense, plain speak that only Joe Kreps could deliver.

"That won't be necessary. I'll meet with them," John relented.

* * * *

It had been some time since John had been on the campus, but it hadn't changed much. The old gymnasium and indoor track, while technologically advanced on the inside, had old brick and ivy on the outside, and still appeared to be missing the same small windows it was twenty years ago. The Yale Bowl, also known as the Shadow's Bowl when he played there, loomed in the not so far off distance.

"Thank you for coming on such short notice," the athletic director said once John sat down in his office. He had been in Pat Leahy's office only one other time in his life—when as the Captain of the football team, he was chewed out for an off campus party some of the players threw which about half the campus had attended.

"Can I get you something to drink?" Leahy asked.

"A water would be great."

Leahy held out an Aquafina.

"I appreciate you asking me to meet with you," John said, feeling as though he should say something.

"I'll be direct, Mann because that's just how I am. Since Coach Gerardi retired two days ago, we've received more than 200 applications via fax, email and snail mail. Some are head coaches at Division III schools with exemplary records. Some are assistant coaches at big time Division I programs. We've even received one from a

Defensive Coordinator in the NFL and another from a retired former NFL coach who won a Super Bowl."

"That's impressive," John admitted. "But then again, it is a pretty good job. There aren't many places better than Yale when you take into account the type of student, tradition and facilities. I imagine it's a rewarding environment to work in."

"Yes, it is. And I'm glad to hear you say that," Leahy added. "Because you're the one we want."

"Excuse me?"

"You're the one we want," Leahy repeated.

"What about Jim Carson?"

Carson had been his running backs coach at Yale, and then his Offensive Coordinator during his brief stint in the NFL.

"He's the head coach of the Browns now. And although we could probably give them a good game, it's still a head NFL job. And to be honest, even if he wanted it, we'd still rather have you."

"I'm flattered. I really am. And don't take this the wrong way, but can I ask why?"

Leahy leaned in for added emphasis. "Because you went here. Because you were like having a coach on the field when you played here. Because you know what the academic workload is like. Because you know the type of kids we attract. Because you know about the traditions. And because people still know you here. You're a legend. You're young and kids will want to play for you. Heck, we've only won the Ivy League title twice since you graduated. But you can resurrect this program. That much I am certain of."

John didn't respond immediately. "I don't know what to say."

"Say you'll do it."

"I'm going to need a day or two to think about it," John said.

He immediately sensed Leahy's disappointment that he didn't jump at the opportunity.

"That's fine. Take a couple days."

"It's not that I don't want the job," John assured him. "I do. It's a just that I have a few things I have to sort out first."

"Another offer?"

"No."

"Well, that's good. Besides, what could be better than coaching at your alma mater? Unless maybe you were named President."

"I think you kind of need to be elected for that to happen."

"You never know. That crazy billionaire James Carr is taking nominations from anyone, anywhere..."

"I read about it. Well, if he calls me, I'll be sure and let you know," John said with a laugh.

John pulled into his driveway an hour later and was surprised to find both Hubbard and Dan Holmes sitting on his porch. If he had been thinking clearly, he might have found it a strange coincidence that they were there together.

"Gentlemen," John said with a nod. "And what are you doing here, Dan? I thought you left?"

"I did. But I'm back."

"What's wrong?" Hubbard asked. "You seem distracted."

"I was offered a job," John explained.

Dan and Hubbard shared a sideways glance.

"No kidding? Doing what?" Dan asked.

"Head Football Coach at Yale."

"No shit?" was Hubbard's response. "Are you going to take it?"

"I have no idea."

Dan realized it was now or never.

"I suppose this is as good a time as any to bring this up."

"Bring what up?"

John fumbled with the lock, and finally opened the door. They walked inside.

"You know the saying, *When it rains, it pours?*" Dan began.

"What about it."

"Well, it's about to start pouring. Job-wise that is."

"Oh really?"

"There's no really easy way to say this, so I'm just going to come right out with it. I don't write for Athletic Administrator Magazine."

"You don't?"

"Have you heard about the Unified Party?"

"Sure. That billionaire banker from Seattle founded it and has begun a nationwide search for a Presidential Candidate. I was just talking about it with the AD from Yale. They're taking nominations from—"

John stopped himself short. Put two and two together and stared at Hubbard, who was uncharacteristically quiet.

"Hubbard...." he admonished.

"Just listen to what he has to say," Hubbard responded.

"Hubbard nominated you, and they sent me down here to see what you were all about," Dan explained.

"You guys must be pretty hard up," John said wryly, with only a hint of a smile.

"Actually, we've got about three truckloads worth of nominations."

"You know Hubbard. I'm sure he did it as a joke."

"I wasn't joking."

"I'm not a politician," John reasoned.

"We don't want a politician."

"I'm just a high school athletic director and football coach."

"Who graduated from Yale," Hubbard said.

"So did 200,000 other people. Why don't you ask one of them?"

"You're bright and personable."

"So was Mr. Rogers."

"You have a good grasp of the issues."

"I'm not an economist."

"You said yourself the economy was cyclical. That it would rise and fall no matter who was in office."

"I was just talking out of my ass to sound impressive."

"You were right."

"I'm not qualified."

"You're the Greatest Mann in the World," Hubbard laughed.

"I'm not even the greatest Mann in my family."

"People would be drawn to you. They would support you. And so would I."

"I'd vote for you too, you goofy bastard," Hubbard added.

When John realized that reasoning was useless, he tried another tact.

"There's no way I could win," he said.

"You don't have to win, to win," Dan reasoned.

John chuckled. "Do you even know what you're saying?"

"You just have earn enough votes to make the party a viable option going forward, and worry the other parties enough so that they both move toward the center—which would be in the best interest of the country."

"I'm not interested in embarrassing myself."

"When I asked you why you've stayed at St. Francis after all this time, you told me, 'Because they need me.'"

"So? I thought you were a reporter at the time and it sounded good."

"You told me that because it was true. But St. Francis doesn't need you anymore. They're doing just fine. The Unified Party does though."

"C'mon. Do you have any idea how ridiculous this sounds?"

"I left a great job with the Democratic National Committee because I wanted to believe in someone again. And I believe in you."

John was out of excuses. He paced across the room and looked out the bay window.

"Promise me you'll at least think about it," Dan asked.

"I'll think about it," John answered after a long pause. How long do I have to decide?"

"We're announcing our candidate Monday morning."

"It's Saturday."

Dan smiled. "Think fast. And I'm sorry for lying to you. I really am. I just wanted to see you in your natural environment. "

John shook his hand.

"Hopefully I'll see you in Seattle in a few days," Dan added.

John slumped into a chair in his living room after Dan had left. Hubbard popped the cap off a beer and handed it to him.

"It's noon," John said.

"You prefer Tequila?" Hubbard asked.

John smiled wryly and took a deep swig.

XX
~HELP FROM AN UNLIKELY SOURCE~

*J*ohn casually flipped through the channels on his television until his eyes settled on the Unified Party symbol on Fox News.

"James Malcolm Carr's new political party is stealing the spotlight early in this election season— at least for the time being as a nation awaits the announcement of its 1ˢᵗ candidate for President," the anchored announced. "The Unified Party is the first party to accept open nominations from anyone, anywhere. Is it a political stunt? Carr has never been known as much of a risk taker. He thinks they can win. The inside word is that they have a short list of five candidates out of the estimated 3.5 million nominations, but they are keeping those names under a deep cloak of secrecy."

Meanwhile, Unified Party headquarters was a beehive of activity. Hundreds of workers manned the phones and gave non-committal answers to those that called every few seconds looking for the inside scoop. Dozens upon dozens of reporters had ascended on the building, camped outside the front door. James, Pat and Dan were seated in a side room. They were excited at the interest they had drawn, but appeared nervous as to how it would all play out.

"Do you think he'll do it?" James asked.

"He'll do it," Dan nodded confidently.

"No one can even find the guy. It's like he's vanished," Pat remarked.

"He said he'd get back to me today."

"And you think he'll accept?"

"I *know* he will," Dan answered.

"What makes you so sure of that?" James asked.

"Because this guy always does the right thing."

"You were with him all of a week," Pat said.

"You could be with him all of a *minute* and be able to tell that," Dan replied.

* * * *

At that very moment, John walked into a bar. It was a secluded, dive bar in Bristol, Connecticut where the locals went to *not* be seen. Erin Jones was already waiting for him in a side booth.

"Thanks for meeting me," John said.

"Of course. It sounded important. Although I have to say I was a bit surprised that I would be the person you'd confide in," she said.

"I'm sorry for dumping this all on you. I just didn't know who else to turn to, and for some reason I thought you could relate."

"What is it?" she asked, her curiosity peaked.

"I've been offered a job. Two of them actually."

"Two jobs?! Well, aren't you Mr. Popular.

So what are they?"

"The first one is that I've been offered the Head Football job at Yale."

Erin shook her head. "I don't like that one."

"Why not?"

"Because I went to Columbia, silly."

"It's my alma mater," John reasoned. "And for the record, I didn't belong to a frat, and I've never been very good at video games, but I did like to drink beer and play poker in college."

"Thanks for telling me you went to Yale, ass."

"Would it have mattered?" he smiled. "I've always had this thing about wanting people to make a judgment about me after they've actually gotten to know me, rather than based on what they've read or heard."

The statement struck a resonant chord with Erin. She had run into that her entire early adult life.

"What's the other offer?" she asked.

"I think you might like that one even less."

"Have to say you have my attention. Are you joining the CIA?"

"No."

"Becoming a terrorist?"

"Uh, no."

"I've got it! You're running for President!" she screamed loudly enough to draw the attention of most of the people in the bar.

When he didn't respond, you could almost see the wheels spinning inside her head.

"You're not really running for President are you?" she said at last. "I mean, I think you're a great guy and all, but..."

"But what?"

"But...I don't know. You're not a politician and I don't see you liking those type of people.

"Maybe that's why I *should* do it."

"You're serious?"

"Have you heard of the Unified Party?"

"That crazy billionaire founded it. They're taking nominations from anyone," she answered followed by a long pause. "Someone nominated you?!"

"Hubbard."

"Gee, there's a real credible person. And they're seriously considering you? They must be pretty hard up. No offense."

"That's what I said."

"I'm just teasing. I think you'd make a great President."

John sensed she was being condescending to him. "Thanks. I think."

"Do I get to be the First Lady?"

"I think we'd have to be married for that to happen."

"Then why don't you start by kissing me and see where it goes?" Erin said playfully.

"I'm serious, here. I don't know what to do," John wailed.

"I was being serious, but ok, ok. Don't have a cow. Let's look at this analytically."

"Ok."

"What are your qualifications?"

"I don't really have any other than being a US citizen who pays his taxes on time. Oh, and I've never smoked pot."

"I don't know that those are necessarily qualifications. I think they're more or less considered pre-requisites. Unless you're Clinton. But they do put you ahead of 75% of the people right off the bat."

"I suppose so."

"Obviously, you're a bright guy," she reasoned. "You went to Yale. What did you study there?"

"Economics."

Erin seemed surprised. "Really? Well, that's a big plus. The economy is a mess. You ever been arrested? Divorced? Missed child support payments? Been with a hooker?"

"No. No. No. And no," John laughed.

"Good. Four more plusses. Look, what really makes someone more qualified than someone else?"

"What do you mean?"

"What I mean is this, I'm sure there are plenty of people that are brighter than some of our past Presidents. And I'm sure that there are plenty of people that are better *people* than some of our past Presidents. So how did they get elected?"

"They ran?"

"Exactly. Everyone has to start somewhere. Someone had to give you your first coaching job."

"Yes, but in coaching, you usually start out as an assistant first."

"Did you?"

"Well, no. But in politics, you usually start out as a Mayor or Governor first."

"Maybe most people do. That doesn't mean you have to. Besides, isn't that kind of the idea behind this new party? To do something different?"

"I suppose. I just don't want to embarrass myself, and be the butt of jokes for late night TV. There's no way I would win."

"If you didn't win, it would only be because people don't know you, and people are distrustful of things they don't know. But you could pave the way for someone else down the road. And how could you possibly embarrass yourself if you're doing something you believe in?"

"So you think I should do it?"

"I didn't say that."

"So you think I shouldn't?"

"I didn't say that either."

"Well, what exactly are you saying?!

"I think I like your first offer better."

"I thought you *didn't* like that one?"

"It's starting to sound better to me."

"Why?"

"You'd get to go back home. Coach where you went to school. Hell, even the weather is nice here now. East is the new West."

"I know. I just hate leaving the kids and people behind at St. Francis. It's a great group of people."

"Well, if you ran for President, you'd be leaving them anyway. So the way I see it, your choice is to stay or leave."

"You're really not much help."

"What do you want me to say?" Erin asked.

"That I don't want you to leave? I don't. I'd like to see how the two of us fared together. And that won't happen if you're in D.C."

"I wouldn't worry too much about that," John said. "It's not like I'd win. Worst case I'd be gone for a few months campaigning, followed by a crushing and humiliating defeat."

"I really doubt that would happen. The crushing and humiliating part I mean. I agree you probably wouldn't win, but how cool would it be to try?"

"I suppose."

"You've got two opportunities of a lifetime in front of you. So yeah, I think you have to take one of them or you'll be kicking yourself for the rest of your life, wondering what could have been."

"I just can't get past the fact that I don't feel deserving of even *running* for President."

"And that's probably what makes you most deserving. You respect the office."

"But still..."

"Some are born great. Others achieve greatness. And some, have greatness thrust upon them," Erin quoted.

"William Shakespeare."

She winked and nodded.

"Did you really mean what you said?" he asked.

"Which part are you referring to?"

"The part about us."

"Of course not. I was joking."

"Oh."

"You're so stupid. In fact, you're probably the dumbest person I know. I'm sure you'd make a great President."

She leaned in and kissed him unexpectedly.

XXI
~AND OUT OF THE DARKNESS~

*T*he clock on the wall read, "11:51am". The crowd outside Unified Party Headquarters had thinned somewhat, but inside, most remained. Waiting. Somewhat impatiently now.

"Pat. You better get Jane Kassidy on the horn," James Carr demanded. "Make sure she's still interested. And see if she can get up here tomorrow. Looks like Dan misread our boy."

Pat nodded somewhat disappointedly. He started entering a number in his cell phone when James stopped him.

"Actually, Pat. Why don't you hold off on that?"

They all turned to look at the back of the room where James was staring and found John Mann standing in the doorway.

"Sun ever shine around these parts?" John asked.

It took a minute for everyone in the room to even realize who he was. Once they did, the volunteer workers stood and applauded their candidate. Dan smiled.

"I'll do it on three conditions," John said as he

handed over a piece of paper.

"What are they?" James asked.

"One. That I get to run on this platform."

John handed over the sheet.

James Carr was not used to people giving him demands, but he was secretly impressed. He began to read it out loud. "1. Campaign Reform. Eliminate fundraising for all campaigns. Candidates should have equal access to TV and newspapers. The two billion dollars spent on your average Presidential campaign could be better spent. 2. Eliminate the two party system and Electoral College. The system is antiquated. There should never be an instance where someone wins the popular vote but loses the election. Everyone's vote should count. It doesn't the way things stand now, which also attributes to low voter turnout."

James nodded in agreement as he continued. "3. All social issues should be handled at the state level.

"I'm talking Marriages. Abortion. Health Care. The Homeless. Legalizing drugs," John interjected. "It is far easier to run social programs for a smaller contingent than an entire country. Running them on the state level would hold all Senators, Governors and Representatives accountable for their actions instead of being able to blame the House, Senate or President. Along that line, institute term limits for Senators, Representatives and Supreme Court Justices. The highest office in the land has a term limit. It's absurd that those offices don't."

"4. Close all tax loopholes," James read.

"If a small business owner tried to run their business without knowing approximately how much income they were bringing in, they wouldn't be in business very long," John reasoned.

"5. Institute a flat tax. 10% Federal. 10% State. 10% on non-essential purchases."

"The wealthy should pay more than the average family. They just shouldn't have to pay a higher *percentage*," John explained. "A family making ten million dollars a year would pay one million in taxes, while a family making one hundred thousand would pay ten thousand in taxes. I'm not a mathematician but I believe that is 990 thousand dollars more in taxes."

"Holy shit, John. Bored on your flight?" Dan laughed.

"There's more," James continued. "6. Fix the housing market and you'll fix the economy. Regulate the banks since they don't appear capable of regulating themselves."

James raised his eyebrow at the implication.

"No offense," John smiled. "Pacific National excluded. Keep interest rates low. If you lose your job, you can have a one time, six month grace period in which you can move your payments to the back of your loan without penalty. If it happens again, the bank agrees to rent the property to you at a lower payment until the house is sold."

"#7," James read. "Give small business owners incentives to hire more people. If the flat tax was 10%, drop it to 5% for companies that take on additional employees. The company would make more net income, unemployment would drop, which would then increase spending. The lost tax income would be made up on non-esstential spending. #8. Regulate all modes of transportation. Airlines. Trains. Buses."

"A seat costs what it costs. Gouging last minute travel discourages spending and travel," John said.

"9. Close the borders," James read.

"People who enter the country illegally should not be allowed to stay. The flip side of that is that people who do things the right way, should be able to obtain their Green Card or citizenship in a much simpler fashion than they do now. Currently, the reverse of this happens."

"And finally...#10. Invade only those who invade us. Being a superpower does have its responsibilities, however, our first obligation should be to ourselves," James finished.

"Wars are costly, and in many instances, never ending. Fight terrorism with stricter safety, tighter immigration laws and greater focus on intelligence, but if someone attacks us on our own soil, come down on them with the force of 1,000 red hot, Arabian suns," John rationalized. "There's more, but I ran out of time."

"I don't really have a problem with any of them," to be honest," James said. "You cross the aisle quite a bit, which could be a good thing. But you said you had three conditions. What are the other two?"

"That I have some say in my running mate.

I'm not saying executive decision making authority, but at least a voice."

"Of course," James answered.

"As long as you don't try to slide Hubbard in there," Dan remarked with a smirk.

"What's the last condition?"

"I am working on a project to house the homeless and need to raise seven hundred thousand dollars quickly," John said.

"Tell me a bit more about it."

"When the weather turned, it left a lot of people on the west coast who were already homeless, in very tough shape. They started coming east where the better weather is, which has created quite a problem. So I've got a friend who owns a couple of buildings in New Haven and is willing to refurbish one of them at his cost and rent out the apartments at a reasonable rate to those in need. My idea is to raise enough money to pay the rent for the entire building for one year to give people enough time to get back on their feet."

James Carr had a look on his face that looked as though he was wondering how he hadn't thought of the idea himself. "We would need to sit down and work out the details, but I like the idea a lot. The money won't be a problem. And not to rush this along too much, but we have to make an announcement in about five minutes. So do we have a deal?"

John smiled as he shook his hand. "Yes. We have a deal."

XXII
~AND THE WINNER IS...~

*J*ohn Mann ran for President. He didn't win, but he won. When the final votes were tallied, he had earned 32% of the vote, good for second place, and good enough to defeat Alan Huber yet again. Huber finished 3rd in what was the highest voter turnout in Presidential election history with 74% of the country voting. The Unified Party became a force on the political landscape, winning ten seats in Congress the following year. Dan Holmes became the Director of Communications and eventually, the Chairman for the party.

With James Malcolm Carr's financial and political backing, John started a program called Project 12—*because 12 months was long enough to change someone's life for the better*—which provided a year of free housing for the homeless in safe neighborhoods, to help them get back on their feet. There were no applications. No sob stories over whose life was worse to determine who received help. It was simply people helping as many people as they could and John always wanted it to remain that way. He wanted someone to be able to walk into an office in a city in Somewhere U.S.A.; ask for help, and receive it.

James and John ran the charity like a Presidential campaign, bringing in enough money to make it the 4th highest grossing charity in the nation. While they were busy raising money, Bernice Kreps did her part to keep the human element in it, overseeing the day-to-day operations from the east coast offices. She still volunteered at a local shelter as well.

Jimmy Davis was soon the highest grossing salesman at Electrical Wholesalers and oversaw the electrical wiring and refurbishing for each building in Project 12. He did that on the side and for free. When John thanked him profusely for his help, Jimmy responded with, "It's the least I could do. I owe you my life," he answered simply.

One day in the future, he would explain to John exactly why that was, but for now, the two of them watched as Project 12 continued to grow. The program quickly expanded to include apartment buildings in Seattle, Los Angeles, Denver, Las Vegas, Chicago, D.C. and Miami.

When December arrived and the first snowflakes of the season began to fall in Los Angeles once again, studio heads scrambled for alternate places to film. They had not been believers in Will's "Push-Pull Theory". Jerry had been the only one proactive enough to start up an East Coast Studio, and as a result, Sunshine Valley was the only major studio likely to have multiple releases out on time for the big July 4th Weekend.

Nick Lawson had benefited as well. He sold his cluster of warehouses and buildings in Hamden, Connecticut to Sunshine Valley for the tidy sum of 52 million dollars. He retired the moment the wire transfer hit his bank account and began "working" as a golf pro at a local country club. He also volunteered at Project 12.

Four days after the Presidential election was complete, John Mann led his Yale football team onto the field as Head Coach. They defeated Harvard for the first time in ten years. Joe Kreps and Eric Holland had been named the interim coaches while John campaigned and stayed on as his Offensive and Defensive Coordinators when he returned. Will Cummings finally got to see what it felt like to run onto a field in front of 80,000 cheering fans after John named him the Academic Liaison for the football program.

And the man who started it all with a simple, uncharacteristically heartfelt nomination? Tom Hubbard inherited his boss's old job and continued to fight with Joe Kovacs daily.

The night after the Yale-Harvard game, twelve people walked into a bar together.

A golf pro.

A movie mogal.

A professor.

A football coach.

A teacher.

A homeless person.

A salesman.

A television reporter.

An investment banker.

An ex-marine.

A speechwriter.

And the greatest Mann in the world.

To an outsider, it may have seemed like an unusual collection of people. But to those involved in the 29 degree tilt, it made all the sense in the world and was an example of life at its finest.

POSTSCRIPT

To me there is no greater character than the unassuming hero. John Mann doesn't have superpowers. He isn't the best looking, or the smartest, or the most athletic. We have all heard of being in the wrong place at the wrong time. Well, John Mann was simply in the right place at the right time; a man who was willing to step forward when everyone else stood still. But before he became *The Greatest Mann in the World*, he was *The Chameleon*—a man whose initial fifteen minutes of fame came from a silly bet. For those that haven't read it, what follows is the first chapter of the story before the story....

"We are like chameleons, we take our hue and the color of our moral character, from those who are around us."

John Locke

THE CHAMELEON

I
~THE BET~

*I*n a world of pushing, shoving, striving-to-get-ahead at all costs people; to those who knew him well, John Mann was a breath of fresh air. His father, however, had always had a differing assessment of him that usually involved a few expletives sandwiched around the four-letter word, "lazy". When his friends described him as the smartest person they knew, his father referred to him as an "enormous waste of god-given ability". The truth, as is usually the case in life, probably lay somewhere in between the two descriptions, although Nick Lawson tended to side more closely with his friends' version; mostly because he was one.

Neighbors since birth, friends shortly thereafter, and classmates since Kindergarten, John and Nick starred together on our high school football and basketball teams, and starred separately on the baseball and golf teams respectively. They were more complements than competitors. If John had a competitor, he came in the form of a self-motivated, egocentric, intellectual named Alan Huber. Although in order to have a competition, there needed to be at least two people competing, and John had no interest in that, which is why he split nearly every award and honor in the school with Alan, instead of hoarding them all to himself. John was number one in the class academically. Alan was number two. Nick was 97th in case you were curious. John was Student Body President. Alan was the President of the debate team. After graduation, Alan went off to study Pre-Law at Harvard. John went off to play football at Yale. Four years later, Alan graduated as the valedictorian of his class, while John graduated as a two-time All-American and the school's all-time leading rusher.

That was where they took two decidedly divergent paths, and where John's father began to develop his rather harsh opinion of him. Alan eventually became the youngest State's Attorney in Connecticut history. Meanwhile, John moved to California and managed a bar in a comfortable little beach town south of Los Angeles, becoming the owner when the original owner passed away and left it to him in his will. It was at that point that John and Nick were reunited after a six year separation, and without meaning to pat himself on the back too heartily, Nick was convinced that if they hadn't been, John would have continued to drift through a life of relative obscurity, succeeding only when success came easily to him—something that was happening less and less frequently as he grew older.

It was twilight by the time Nick finished the 15 minute ride from LAX to Hermosa Beach, and dozens of volleyball players scrambled to finish their matches before dark. Hundreds of people were also walking along the Strand—the 25 mile bike and walking path that connected Redondo

Beach to Malibu—some to relax after a long day at work, others to continue what had already been a relaxing day.

Facing the clear blue ocean a mere few feet from the sandy courts of pro beach volleyball's most prestigious tournament, *The Shanty* was the definition of a dive beach bar. No matter how many times John had described it to Nick over the phone, he always felt as though he was exaggerating its' deficiencies—until he stepped into the place for the first time. It had tall, well-worn oak tables and stools both inside and on the covered patio outside. Stains and carvings on them were more the norm than the exception, as if it was encouraged, and more sand was visible on the floor than hardwood. The sign above the entrance read, "NO SHIRT, NO SHOES, NO PROBLEM".

The typical crowd in the bar was one of the more eclectic and diverse ones around. There were the local barflies bellied up to one end of the bar, while a few shirtless pro beach volleyball players shared a pitcher at the other end. A collection of wannabe actors and actresses convened at a large table in the middle of the room, arguing over the merits of the newest batch of television shows they were not a part of. In the far corner, an actual successful actor who was only in *The Shanty* so he could spend a night in relative anonymity, sat with two friends. Also in the bar at 6:00pm on your typical Tuesday night in November, were three of the most stunning women Nick had ever laid eyes on. Their six foot statures and bikini bottoms indicated that they had just stepped in for a drink from the volleyball courts. Most of the men in the bar were far too intimidated to even speak to them. Either that, or they were realistic enough to know that these women were clearly out of their league. But there was always *one* guy with unwarranted confidence. A good looking guy, who had been a great looking guy a few years back, but hadn't yet come to terms with the fact that he wasn't twenty-five anymore. Steve Abbott was now thirty-something, and carrying a few extra pounds on a frame that was topped off with a tussle of dark hair. He got up from the table of wannabes and marched over to the young ladies in question.

"You know what would look good on you?" he asked one of them.

She cringed at the response she knew was coming.

"Me," he continued.

She rolled her eyes and looked away. Undaunted, Abbott turned to one of her friends as if she was part of a to-do list. "That's a great bikini. I bet it would look even better crumpled up next to my bed in the morning."

"Weak," the girl responded.

He turned to the third one. "So how about a pizza and a fuck?"

With no hesitation, she slapped him across the face with the force of a Serena Williams forehand, before all three walked away.

"What?!" he yelled after her, "you don't like pizza?! We can eat something else!"

With his easy smile, Hawaiian shirt, cargo shorts and Banana Republic flip flops, the man behind the bar looked even more relaxed and casual than Nick had remembered him, "Could you try not to chase off all the women in the place?" John Mann said.

"I don't see any women in here," Abbott responded, looking around.

"Not anymore," John laughed before he noticed Nick standing ten feet away. "Holy crap," he continued as he hurdled the bar with the ease of a pommel horse medalist. "As I live and breathe. Nick Lawson. What are *you* doing here?!"

"I got tired of the snow and cold weather," Nick answered.

"Are you visiting or moving here?"

"Moved."

"Do you have a job?"

"Nope. But from what I can see, no one seems to work much out here anyway."

"Do you need a place to stay?"

"Nope."

"Where are you staying?"

"With you," Nick said matter-of-factly.

"What makes you think that's an option?" he smiled.

"Because you need me out here."

"And why is that?"

"Because someone has to prevent you from throwing yourself into the Pacific."

"Now why would I do that?"

Nick pointed at the television.

"It's all over in Connecticut," Fox News Anchor, Megyn Kelly said, "as a Democrat has been elected the youngest Governor in United States history.   At thirty-three years and seven months, Alan Huber has defeated Ron Baldelli by a margin of 52 to 48 percent."

"I'm happy for him," John replied, feigning indifference.

"Huber was John's biggest rival in high school," Nick explained to the men seated at the bar. "They were number one and two in the class academically. John was number one. Huber was Student Body President. John was President of the Varsity Club. Huber went to Harvard. John went to Yale—"

The older of the two men at the bar interjected, "And now he's a Governor and John's a bartender."

"I'm not just a bartender. I'm the owner," John answered.

"You own this shithole? I always thought you were just helping out a friend to pick up a little cash."

"If this place is such a shithole, how come you're in here all day, every day?"

"Because I can't afford to go to a nice place."

"Fair enough," John laughed. "And no matter what you guys all think, I wish Alan well."

"A tale of two lives," Nick said. "Does it ever bother you that you've failed to do more with the abilities God gave you?"

"You sound like my father."

Nick had always been good at pushing John's

buttons. "I'm here because I want to be here," he continued. "I like my life. I don't ever have to put on a suit and tie except for weddings and funerals. I make an ok living meeting colorful people. I don't have anyone to tie me down. I'm a lone wolf. Howling at the moon."

"You're here because you can't work for anyone else. You've either been fired or walked off of every other job you've had. And if by "ok living meeting colorful people", you mean hanging out with drunks and bar flies, while making slightly above minimum wage, then yes, I agree. And you don't have anyone to tie you down because you have serious commitment issues. As for that lone wolf thing....I'll give you that one," Nick answered.

"That Huber guy must have a lot going for him. He'll probably be President some day," the older man at the bar offered.

Abbott was smiling behind John. He knew they had him going now.

"Oh, he's had plenty going for him," John began. "He got into Harvard because his father built the library. He got into Harvard Law because his uncle went to college with the Dean. And after dating the Dean's ugly daughter for four years, the Dean then got him the job in the State Attorney's Office. As for the election, his family had 100 times more money than the other candidate."

"So you're saying the only reason he's successful, is because of the advantages he's had?" Nick asked.

"I'm saying that *anyone* with his advantages

would be Governor right now."

"Interesting," Abbott said. "I smell a bet coming on."

"What kind of bet?" John inquired.

Nick thought it over. "So you think with certain advantages, you could do anything and be successful?"

"Anything within reason."

"Ok. I'm just free-flowing ideas here, but how bout this. We pick ten occupations. From that list, you have to choose five of them. You'll have a maximum of six months to succeed at each. We'll give you every advantage you need to help you get the jobs."

"What kind of advantages can you guys give me?" John asked skeptically.

"I know a lot of people," Abbott said.

"I'm not sure I want to know the people you know."

"I'm serious. Anything goes," Nick told him. "You can lie on your resume. Cheat. Beg. Borrow. Steal. Call in favors. Whatever you need to do to get the job. After that, it will be performance based."

"What kind of jobs are we talking about?"

"Nothing that would require years of training or would jeopardize peoples' lives. Nothing like an air traffic controller or Neurosurgeon. But high profile jobs. Jobs that everyone always assumes they can do better than the people that do them."

"Like a weather man?"

"Exactly."

"What else?"

"Like I said, I'm just thinking out loud here. You've got to give us a couple of days to come up with the list. We can really amp it up. Publicize the hell out of it. Pack this place the night you pick the jobs."

"Speaking of this place..." John said. It was clear he was giving it some thought. "Who would run it, while I was off doing these jobs?"

"I would," Nick answered. "I need a job."

"I'll help him," Abbott offered.

"You'd drink all the profits," John responded.

"That's the price of chasing glory, my friend," Abbott said.

"And how do I win?"

"You win by not getting fired, and by doing your job better than the average person would do it. If you were a cab driver in New York City, you'd have to pull in more than the average driver on that route would. I'm not saying that would be one of the jobs. That's just an example. We'd have to evaluate on a case by case basis once you decide which ones you're going to do," Nick explained.

"What are the stakes?"

"What do you want them to be?"

"50 grand."

"50 grand?!! That's a little steep."

"I could be giving up over a year of my life."

"Your life isn't that great," Abbott deadpanned.

"Besides, you'd be getting paid to do it," Nick interjected. "Handsomely in some instances.

Plus, you'd have income from the bar and probably a book deal by the time you were done."

"Not if I'm in jail."

"They don't arrest you for lying on your resume. They fire you."

"How about this? We start with 50 grand if it takes a year, but if it takes six months, it's only 25 grand. If it takes six WEEKS, then a percentage— like $5,700."

I thought it over. "Tell you what," Nick said. "Let's pack this place Thursday night. Make it an underground event because we don't want it to end up in the papers. We give 'em some food. 150 bucks a person. If we get 300 people, there's 45 grand, regardless of how long it takes."

The old man at the bar chimed in. "Put me down for a hundred-fifty."

"You already owe 400 on your tab," John responded.

"Then make my tab 550. I want in on this."

"And if I lose?"

"I didn't think that would be a possibility in your mind," Nick smiled.

"It's not really, but...every bet has to have stakes on both sides."

"How about if you lose, we throw an All-Day, Open Bar party here at *The Shanty* on you," Abbott suggested.

John nodded with no hesitation. "Ok." He shook both of our hands. "It's a deal."

ABOUT THE AUTHOR

MATT MICROS received a B.A. in American Studies from the University of Notre Dame and his M.S. in Television, Radio and Film from Syracuse's Newhouse School of Communications, before spending nearly a decade in Los Angeles working in television production. He followed with a stint at Creative Artists Agency before returning to the east coast. *The Greatest Mann in the World* is his 5th novel, and the sequel to 2014's *The Chameleon*. Matt currently resides in Stratford, Connecticut with his wife, Katy, and their yellow and black labs, Mr. Beans and Mr. Bode.

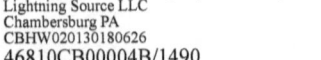